THE AWAKENING

MICHAEL F. LAWRENCE JR.

Acknowledgements

When the idea of writing my book first came up, I thought to myself this is a crazy idea and that no one would want to read it. The idea that crosses one's mind when taking a risk on themselves. This section of my book is dedicated to the ones who saw my passion, my creativity, and my love for creating this amazing book. First giving thanks to spirit and the creator, for being with me throughout my entire journey. For assisting me in finding the love and creativity that was always inside of me. Thank you to my friends, who stayed on me constantly during this process. Thank you to my family and loved ones who supported me and my vision. Thank you to my spiritual brothers and sisters for knowledge, love and inspiration on my journey. Finally, most importantly, thank you to this amazing reader who took the time to pick up this book. I am beyond grateful and thankful for everyone reading this book. I send you love, blessings, positive energy, and hope that this book leaves something deep inside of you to help you find a piece of you that loves you more than anything else in this world. Much Love!

Find your Passion, Follow your Purpose, Stay on your Path

Asé

TABLE OF CONTENTS

PROLOGUE

The master and his apprentice sat down on the warm soft sand, gazing into the mighty blue sea. Listening to the waves roar, as they crashed into the land.

"When was the last time you've seen the ocean?" the master asked.

The young apprentice looked far out into the sea, gazing at its beauty.

"I've never seen the ocean master…It's looks so beautiful… peaceful…and calming" said the apprentice.

The master smiled, placed his hands into the sand and brought the sand up, watching it fall slowly through his fingers.

"The ocean is one example of pure balance within nature my young apprentice… From the waves of the ocean waters... to the wind in the air that surrounds it…to the warm sand that sits at the edge…to the birds that fly above it, and the fish that swim in it… they are all connected and at balance."

As the master and apprentice observed the ocean, the apprentice began to feel something from deep within his spirit. A chill began to move from the bottom of his spine to the top of his head. He continued to stare out into the ocean but he knew what this energy was.

"Master…Why exactly are we here?" asked the apprentice.

The master looked up into the bright blue sky and began to smile.

"My young apprentice…when one book is coming to a close, another shall begin to open" said the master.

The apprentice turned and looked at his master,

"…meaning?" asked the apprentice.

With another smirk on his face, the master replied.

"My book and my life have finally come to a close. All of my teachings, all of my knowledge and all of my wisdom I pass on to you... I must now journey into the cosmos and be one with the universe."

The apprentice turned away and again stared off into the ocean. Taking in the words of his master, the apprentice began to shed tears from his eyes.

"Why the tears my young apprentice?" asked the master.

"Because... I am hurt!" yelled the apprentice! "There is so much I want to know. Many things I have yet to learn from you, and now...you're just leaving me...to be alone..."

The master placed his hand on the head of the apprentice.

"Aww my dear boy...you are growing into a young man now. You have so much light and knowledge inside of you...but it is only when I am gone that you will be able to become the best version of yourself" said the master.

The apprentice began wiping away his tears and opened his ears to his masters words.

"As humans we fear change...we fear loneliness, and we fear the thought of letting go...but it is in those times, we must find the light and strength within to grow into the spiritual beings we were made to be."

The apprentice looked up into the sky as the birds began to fly by. The ocean waves began to roar louder and louder. The dolphins began jumping into the air and from a very long distance, a mighty blue whale breached into the sky and crashed back into the water.

"My apprentice...you are stronger my boy. You will grow to help many people in this world...but in order to do that I must leave, so you can grow. You won't understand now, or tomorrow, or even in the years to come...but when you do, only then will you understand the true power of your gift and your purpose" said the master.

The apprentice looked at his master and took his words to heart.

The master looked out into the ocean and began

to smile again.

"The beauty of looking at nature and being at peace. A happiness that no one can take from you my apprentice. If you ever are in need…go out into nature…stand in the sun or even the moon…and close your eyes…you'll find, that I'm always with you…"

The Master and the apprentice sat on the beach, gazing at the water and sky for hours, until the sun began to set. As the night sky took over, the light of the moon began to touch the ocean. As the ocean waves began to calm, the master's presence began to fade. With the night came stars that lit up the sky, and the beauty of the moon shone bright upon the entire land and ocean. The apprentice looked to the side, where his master had been sitting. There was nothing left but the garments and robe that the master left behind. His spirit had taken journey on into the cosmos and the night sky. The apprentice stood up in the cold sand, gathering the things his master had left behind. Before he began his walk home, he turned and looked up into the night sky. He closed his eyes, smiled and said with a whisper,

"Thank you."

CHAPTER 1

THE UNBALANCED MAN

"And there I was standing in front of this giant pyramid, gazing at its golden beauty, as the moon shined down on top of it. Then … I woke up, and that was my dream. Now I know what you're going to say, and no I did not make all of this up to change the subject of what we were supposed to talk about today. I simply…changed the subject of what we were supposed to talk about today to avoid answering all questions."

Laying down on a couch, staring at the ceiling, is a young man by the name of Virgil Harris. Virgil is a 27-year-old African American male, from the very small town of LaGrange, Ga. He was born the night of December 5th, 1992, on a very cold Saturday, to his parents Mr. and Mrs. Harris. Mrs. Harris knew her son was going to be special because the moon's light, shining bright from the sky, was beaming through the hospital window right onto him. For the first nine years of his life, Virgil was what you would call, a black sheep. He was different, in his own natural intriguing way. He had a habit of talking to himself a lot and playing scenarios in his head at random times. He found it very difficult to communicate with others or to make friends unless it was on the topics of anime, cartoons, movies or videogames. Other kids saw him as an odd person. When Virgil tried to talk or make friends they tended to, well, make fun of him. Once he lost his control of his emotions and temper which lead him to exploding into a fight with other kids. The kids constantly made fun of how he talked, dressed and just for how he looked. He tried to open up to his parents about it but they did not understand him. However, there was one kid he became really close with, and even became best friends with. Virgil finally had a friend, but that changed when his parents decided to move and start a new life in a different town shortly after. Virgil ended up spending the rest of his childhood and teenage years trying to make new friends and opening up....it didn't work out so well. By this time his twin little sisters had been born Lia and Nia. He called them the spawn of evil. Virgil experienced constant fights, arguments and unnecessary unharmful torture from his sisters and since he never established a true connection with his parents either, he felt like he couldn't express himself he caught consequences from them as well. He eventually just stayed to himself.

Virgil finally reached high school where he met and experienced his first love. He had never felt this feeling of love or happiness before. Which, over time, made him happy. Their relationship lasted for quite some time but then college came, and they went their separate ways. From that point he started searching for a new woman so that he could feel love again...that feeling of being important. Well...that did not work out so well. After several attempts, there seemed to be nothing but failure at the end. After several years of stress, anger and emotional unbalance Virgil's parents forced him to see a therapist.

"...Well then, that did not turn out as expected" said the therapist.

"Why are we avoiding the discussion of today Virgil?"

The young man continued to stare into the ceiling.

"The last thing I want to think about today, Doctor Coleman, is everything going on in my life right now. It really doesn't matter to me. My dreams are all that matter right now."

Doctor Coleman closed her notepad, placed it on her desk and smiled.

"Okay, let's talk about these dreams then" she said.

Virgil turned his head and looked at Dr. Coleman.

"Now about these dreams, tell me about them."

There was a brief moment of silence between the two.

"I've…been dreaming about standing in front of this giant pyramid…It's bright and golden from the moons reflection… I'm standing right in front of it, reaching for it. It's like…it's calling me, but I can never get to it. The harder I reach for it…the sand below my feet keeps pulling me away… Then I look on top of the pyramid, and there's this figure standing on top of it… just watching me trying to reach for the pyramid… Then I wake up…"

Virgil turns, looks upward towards the ceiling and closes his eyes. Doctor Coleman took a moment to gather her thoughts.

"So, this figure, it just watches you struggle to reach this pyramid?"

Virgil sits up from the couch and folds his arms.

"Yea, it's a bright figure and I can tell it's a person… it's been the same in every dream for the last few weeks now."

Doctor Coleman sat back in her chair and folded her arms.

"It seems to me Virgil that, you feel someone, or something is watching you struggle to get to your goal. Which in this aspect, the goal is the giant pyramid…have you ever tried asking that figure for help in your dream?"

Virgil shook his head "No, I've never thought about it… I'm good at figuring things out on my own…Never really had to ask anyone for help. I'd rather help others than receive help."

"Awee! So we're getting somewhere" said Doctor Coleman.

"You've been coming to see me for, awhile now and this is some great knowledge Virgil."

"It is?" asked Virgil, with the look of confusion on his face.

"Indeed!" said Doctor Coleman. "In our last few sessions, you've shared that you feel stuck and lost in life. From not having the career you wanted, to recently going through a breakup and from feeling hopeless form seeing others success."

"What exactly does any of that have to do with my dreams?" asked Virgil.

"Well, tell me if I'm wrong. You do not like receiving help from anyone it seems. You tend to take on your life alone and figure it out yourself. Correct?" asks Doctor Coleman

Virgil turned his head and looked off to the side, "Sure, I guess."

"It seems Virgil, this thing wants you to ask for help, but only if you will allow it to help you.

Maybe, it wants to help you get to your goal or goals" said Doctor Coleman.

"Honestly" said Virgil, while focusing his attention towards Doctor Coleman.

"I don't have any goals at the moment... except make money, find a new potential girlfriend and be happy... Money, love, happiness, that's it."

Dr. Coleman and Virgil made eye contact while sitting in silence for a few minutes.

"Well... you came to me for help, so I know you have something deeper in you that wants the help" says the therapist.

"Nah, I'm okay" said Virgil. "I honestly just come here for my parents and family. They're concerned and I don't need them worrying about me. Now I just need some more time to myself, I'm no longer in the mood to open up about my life right now."

Virgil began putting his shoes on and gathering his things.

"Virgil" said Doctor Coleman while looking into his eyes. "I believe in you...there is something very special about you, but only you have to be able to see that...I am here for you and support you."

Virgil smirked, and began to walk to the door. "Thank you, I appreciate that."

Virgil exited the therapist office and began walking to his car. Virgil, with his head looking down, began to think and reflect on the therapist words.

"Me? Special?... no, there's nothing special about me...I'm just average."

Virgil, with his head still done, pulls out his keys to his car. All of a sudden, he accidently bumped into the person passing by him, dropping his keys in the motion.

"Oh, my bad, I was not paying attention at all. I apologize" said Virgil.

The strange person walking by happened to be an older African American man, who looked barely over the age of sixty. Standing about six feet tall, wearing what seemed to be a black and white designer long-sleeved shirt, with white pants. With him, on his shoulder, was a black and white cat.

"It's not a problem at all young man, but you should definitely start walking with your head held up and not down" said the older man.

The cat, that was on the man's shoulder hopped down and onto the ground. It walked over to Virgil and grabbed the keys that had been dropped. The cat walked back over to the older man, with the keys. The older man leaned down and the cat hopped back on to his shoulder, dropping the keys in the older man's hand.

"That's a very smart and loyal cat you have there" said Virgil.

The man laughed, stood back up tall, and handed Virgil his keys.

"Kema? She's only kind when she chooses to be but don't test her kindness" said the man.

Virgil smirked and grabbed his keys from the man. As the man began to turn and walk, Virgil noticed a strange necklace around the man's neck.

"Wait..." said Virgil.

The man stopped and turned around.

"What's that necklace around your neck?" asked Virgil.

The man looked down his neck and grabbed the

necklace.

"Oh, this?" said the man. "This is a very special necklace, made by a very special dear to me. I cannot personally tell you what it is. Just know it's very special."

Virgil walked up to the man and observed the necklace. The necklace was circular with a black and gold color. Inside the circle were seven different color crystal like stones. The stones seemed to be attached to branches which led to a tree. In the center of the tree, sat an eye and on the top of the necklace sat the head of a cobra.

"You seem very interested in this necklace young man." Said the old man.

"I am, it's interesting and very mysterious" said Virgil. "It's as if I've seen it before somewhere."

The man smirked and placed the necklace back on his chest.

"I have a shop right outside of town, right next to a Japanese ramen restaurant. You come out there and I can craft one up for you. I'll be there tomorrow afternoon working on another project. Come by if you are still interested" said the old man.

"Most definitely." said Virgil.

They shook hands and both went on their way. Virgil walked to his car, hopped in and drove of home. As Virgil drove off in the direction towards home, he passed by the old man and his cat. The old man stood on the corner of the street, next to a floral shop right beside the office of Virgil's therapist. The man watched Virgils car drive off, out of the city. The man turned and looked at his cat.

"Tell me Kema, do you believe he's ready now?"

The cat looked up at the old man and meowed.

"Hmmm, interesting...follow him, watch over him and bring him to me tomorrow." The cat jumped off of the old man's shoulder and began walking in the direction of Virgils car.

"So...the time has finally come" said the old man.

The old man proceeded into the floral shop.

Virgil lives in the small town of LaGrange, Georgia. He stays on the outskirts of the city in a medium size two-bedroom apartment. On his way home, Virgil stopped by the nearest fast food restaurant and grabbed him dinner for the night.

While driving home, he again reflected on his meeting with his therapist. Virgil arrived home and walked into his apartment. Once inside he walks into the living room area, placed his book bag onto a sofa cushion and his keys, wallet, cell phone and dinner onto the living room table. He then fell onto the couch and lets out a long sigh. From the rear of his apartment one of the bedroom doors opens up. Cole, Virgil's cousin and roommate, walks into the living room.

"What's up bro?!" Cole asked walking into the kitchen area.

Virgil lifts his head up from the couch.

"I bought a spicy chicken sandwich, with a large French fry and a side of chicken nuggets. Now I need several beers, a small container of cookie dough ice cream and a full day of nothing but videogames" said Virgil.

Virgil slowly face palms back into the couch.

Cole looks at Virgil making a side gesture face at him.

"Bro...really?"

Virgil sat up on to the couch

"Yep I'm hungry, stressed, tired of working a pointless job, tired of feeling like I have absolutely no control of where I am going anymore in life...oh and my love life sucks."

Cole laughed, shakes his head and walks over to the refrigerator. He opened the fridge, grabs two bottles of spring water.

"Virgil, look man everything is a process. What fun would life be if everything was just handed to us."

Cole walked over into the living room and sat the bottle of spring water in front of Virgil. "I definitely said a cold beer" say's Virgil.

Cole begins to walk back to his room, "I know but what kind of cousin would I be if I gave you what you wanted? Especially with the already crappy food you're eating now."

Cole walked off into his bedroom and closes the door. Virgil sat up on the couch, grabbed his food, the remote to the tv and the video game controller.

"Dinner and videogames for one? Absolutely."

Virgil turned the tv and game on, opened his food and began to eat. The night slowly began to set, and in the blink of an eye the day was over. Virgil looked down at his phone to check the time.

"Are you serious! It's midnight already! I gotta get some sleep."

Virgil hopped up off the couch and turned everything off. He grabbed all of his things and threw away his trash. He headed to his bedroom and started his nightly routine with a quick hot shower. Afterwards he puts on a black t shirt and a pair of basketball shorts. He sat on his bed, threw some lotion on his skin, turns all the lights off and laid down to attempt to fall asleep. As sleep slowly began to set in, Virgil slowly closed his eyes and wandered off. From Virgils bedroom window, the moon began to shine through a slight opening in the window blinds. Within the moons bright light appeared a figure of a cat. The cat laid next to the window and looked in between the slight opening of the window blinds to find Virgil asleep. The cat laid their and watched over the young man and when night turned to dawn it disappeared.

PT. 2

THE OLD MAN'S CHALLENGE

The sun slowly began to rise, and light shined through the window of Virgils bedroom. The alarm from Virgils cell phone began to ring. Virgil slowly turned over, grabbed his phone, sitting on his nightstand, and hit the snooze button.

"Ten more minutes, I promise" said Virgil.

The light from the sun began to shine brighter in Virgils room. Virgil rolled over to grab his phone again but this time it was gone.

"Huh..where did..where did my phone go?"

Virgil sits up from his bed to look for his phone. The phone began to sound the alarm again but from the front of the room this time. Virgil turned his attention to the front in confusion and found the phone now on the computer desk. Virgil got out of bed to grab his is phone. As he approached his phone he heard a calm "meow" come from behind him. Virgil turned around and was shocked to find a black and white cat sitting on his bed.

"Where did you come from?!"

The cat eased down onto Virgils bed and closed it's eyes. Virgil now in confusion grabbed his phone, walked to the window to check for any openings and out into the living room area. His cousin Cole was sitting on the couch working on his computer.

"Ummm, Cole, did you happen to leave any doors or windows open last night?" Cole looked up at Virgil in confusion.

"Uhhh, noo. I woke up, went for a run and did some yoga on the patio but I didn't leave anything open. Why? Whats up?" asked Cole.

Virgil now looking even more confused.

"Okay bro there's a cat in my room on my bed."

Both Cole and Virgil walk into the bedroom to find nothing there.

"Impossible" said Virgil.

He looked under the bed, and all throughout his room but no cat was found.

"It was just here, I promise bro" says. Virgil.

Cole laughs "Bro it's too early for this. It's 7:30am and I have a lot of work to do."

Virgil looks at Cole with a side face gesture.

"All you do is watch stocks and trade Cole."

Cole nods his head in agreeance.

"Exactly, and there's money to be made today."

Cole walks back into the living room, while Virgil still stands in disbelief.

"Wait…did you say 7:30!!" yells Virgil.

Virgil, realizing the time, rushed to brush his teeth, get dressed and rushed out the door. As Virgil rushes towards his car, he begins to notice something very small laying on the roof of his car. It's the black and white cat again.

"How did it get out here?!"

Virgil walks up to the car and the cat opens its

eyes while slightly lifting its head. Both Virgil and the cat stared back at each other in silence.

"I don't have time for this, and I'm already late for work. I'm going to need you to move."

The cat continued to stare back and then slowly laid its head back down on to the car.

Virgil walks to car and shouts at the cat.

"Get off my car!!!"

The cat slowly lifts its head again. Stands up, looks at Virgil and slowly walks off of the car. It jumps down on to the ground, then jumps back up onto the car next to Virgils and lays back down. Virgil, now in awe, opens his car door

"See...that's why the mouse was my favorite growing up in cartoons."

Virgil hops in the car, turns on the ignition and begins heading toward his job. As the car drives off, the black and white cat lifts its head to see the direction of the car. It stands up and slowly begins to walk in the same direction.

Virgil works at an Elementary School as a paraprofessional. With a bachelor's in physical education and master's in counseling, he hopes to one day possibly move up and become a teacher or counselor. Despite his dislike for waking up early, and not making enough money, he gets up every morning for only one reason, to help and support his students. Virgil pulled up to his school and rushed into work. As Virgil walks inside the school building, he is met by his principal.

"You were almost late again today Mr. Harris" said the principal.

"I apologize, I have a lot going on and I'm working on doing better" said Virgil.

The Principal looked at Virgil and shook her head.

"I'm going to need you to do better and step it up Mr. Harris. You have way too much potential to be this way."

Virgil nodded his head and went on his way.

The day went by and Virgil did his job like he does every day. He met with teachers. He worked with students in small groups and he avoided overworking. When the final bell ringed Virgil gathered his things, said goodbye to his students and walked to his car. As Virgil approached his car, a familiar friend was waiting on him.

"You again" said Virgil.

On the hood of his car sat the black and white cat, waiting for him to arrive. Virgil walks up to the cat.

"Look, I apologize for yelling at you this morning but why are you bothering me so much??" asked Virgil.

The cat meowed and continued to look at Virgil. Virgil took a closer look at the cat and saw it had a collar with the name Kema on it.

"Kema?.. you're that old man's cat from yesterday? Am I really that slow to not ever notice this, this whole time?" Virgil said to himself.

"Well, I don't know why exactly you've been following me but lucky for you I am heading to see your owner now."

Virgil grabbed Kema, placed her in the passenger seat of his car and drove off. Virgil looked over at Kema, "don't move or scratch anything okay? Just sit there! I just cleaned my car out."

The cat looked at Virgil, stretched, hopped in his lapped and laid down.

"I really don't do cats" said Virgil.

He picked Kema up and placed her back in the passenger seat of the car. The cat again stood up and hopped back into Virgils lapped.

"Why are you tormenting me like this?" asked Virgil.

The cat meowed and laid down in his lapped as he continued to drive to the old mans shop. Virgil pulled up to the Japanese ramen restaurant right outside of town but there was nothing else there.

"That's very weird" said Virgil.

He pulled up to a parking spot and parked his car. Virgil picked up Kema and got out of the car. He placed Kema on the ground and walked up to the ramen restaurant. He looked around the area and there was no other building in site. Kema mowed from behind him and began walking towards the front door of the ramen restaurant. Virgil opened the door and they both walked inside. The inside of the ramen restaurant was very different from many. The lighting was very dim but enough to see the area. The tables were rounded, closer to the ground and in the middle of each table was a small fountain of running water with an unlit incense on top. There were soft medium sized pillows on the ground instead of chairs and the best part, not many people were there.

"How may I help you sir?" Virgil turned and saw a short Asian woman, behind a counter, smiling back at him.

"Oh…ummmm, I'm looking for a tall, black old guy. Grey hair, dresses semi fancy. He's supposed to have a shop right next door" said Virgil.

"Ah yes, he's been expecting you. Right this way please."

The woman walked around the counter and lead Virgil to the back of the restaurant. She led him outside to an area surrounded by bamboo plants. The was only one sitting area and it was underneath a small cherry blossom tree. The table was larger and rectangular with a large waterfall fountain in the middle. Medium pillows were placed right in front of the table. At the top of the table sitting right in front of the cherry blossom tree sat the old man drinking some tea.

"Ahh you've finally arrived, it took you long enough" said the old man.

The woman sat Virgil right next to the old man, while Kema walked over and hopped in the old man's lap.

"Would you like any tea sir?" asked the woman.

"Yes, he would" the old man answered.

Virgil nodded his head at the woman, and she walked back into the restaurant.

"I don't drink tea" said Virgil.

"Ohh, this is ginseng tea, very good for you. You'll love it" said the old man.

Virgil looked down at Kema and back up at the old man.

"Sooo, I thought you owned a craft shop?" asked Virgil.

"Oh, I do, it's right behind this beautiful cherry blossom tree. I needed a drink of tea before I returned back to work. I haven't forgotten about our chat from yesterday."

The old man picked up his cup of tea and took

a sip. Virgil started to fell suspicious about the old man.

"Anyways, why was your cat following me all day today?" asked Virgil.

The old man laughed and took another sip of his tea

"Because I asked her to" said the old man.

Virgil look at the old man in confusion.

"Why would you have a cat follow me all day?" asked Virgil.

The old man placed his cup of tea down in front of him.

"To make sure you made it here with no excuses. She's a very intelligent and spiritual being. She's been waiting for this moment for a long time" said the old man.

"Excuse me...a long time? What are you talking about?" asked Virgil

"Virgil, my young friend, Kema has been following you since you were a young boy. It's just recently that you've noticed her because she made herself noticeable yesterday. We've both have been waiting for this day" said the old man.

Virgil was beginning to feel very uneasy and his suspicion continued to grow.

"I never told you what my name was" said Virgil.

"Ohh, so you're only shocked because I know your name. I know very, very many things about you Virgil Harris. You were born December 4th, 1992 from your mother Shae Harris and your father Frederick Harris. You were the only child, and you grew up spoiled for nine years until your younger twin siblings sisters were born. When you and your family moved to a new location, because of your fathers new job, you became closed in and sheltered. You found it very hard to make new friends and you suffered from bullying because you were different from the rest of the children. Since your parents were always tired from working and taking care of you and your sisters you became closed off from the world. Hurt because they never really showed you any more attention. You stayed to yourself, and always remained in your room. As long as you had your videogames, music and anime you were content. Deep down inside, however, you yearned for love, acceptance and attention. The older you got you became interested in love and started to date many girls because you thought it would bring you happiness. By the way one of those girls I really did not like for you at all. Anyways, you became older and began trying to find ways to make you happy and to feel loved. You tried to fix and please everyone you came in contact with. You always wanted validation and felt like you needed to prove yourself to someone. You never learned to set boundaries and you always de-prioritized your own needs. Now here you are at age twenty seven going through a life crisis in every area. How did all of that sound? Familiar?" said the old man.

Virgil was stunned and frightened at the same time. No one, not even his close friends never knew all of that about him. Not even his parents. Who was this old man and how did he know so much? The Asian waitress walked out from the restaurant up to Virgil and the old man.

"Here is your cup of tea sir and here is a tea pot if you would like more" said the waitress.

"Thank you, my friend," said the old man.

Virgil still stunned could not even find the

words to say anything or express how he was feeling.

"You should drink some tea Virgil, it will help with the shock and calm your nerves" Said the old man.

"Old man, I don't know who you are or how you know so much about me but It's very uncomfortable so.. I think I'm just going to go. Thanks for the necklace offer but I'm going to have pass."

Virgil stood up to his feet and began walking towards the restaurant door.

"Virgil...I wouldn't do that if I were you."

Virgil stopped and look back at the old man.

"Old man, there is nothing you could possibly say to get me to stay here after all you just told me."

"Oh really?" said the old man with a smirk on his face.

Virgil began to turn around and walk towards the door.

"What if I told you I could help you fix all of those problems that you are facing better and reveal how I know so much about you?" said the old man.

As Virgil began to reach for the door he stopped and slowly turned around.

"Ahhh, that got your attention I see. Now come on back over and have some tea. Cold tea is great but it's nothing great like fresh hot tea."

The old man took another sip from his cup.

Virgil walked back over to the old man and stood next to him.

"I'm listening, you have 5 minutes" said Virgil.

"I have a proposal for you my young friend. More so a challenge for you" said the old man.

Virgil standing next to the old man, folds his arms and remains in confusion.

"Why exactly should I accept this challenge and what does it have to do with you helping me?" asked Virgil.

The old man took another sip of his tea.

"You have two choices Virgil. The first choice, you can walk out that door back to the front of the restaurant. The moment you step out into the front of that building, all of this that I'm telling you and us meeting will never have happened to you. It will be wiped from your memory clean. You can go about your life trying to figure things out alone and by yourself, like you have been doing."

The old man picked up the tea pot and poured more tea into his cup.

"The second choice, you can finally take a risk and invest into yourself. You can have a seat and drink some tea with me. I will take you under my wing as my student or some would say apprentice. I will teach you the ways of obtaining amazing physical and mental health. I will guide you and take you on a journey through your spirit to find the areas where you have blockage. Finally, at the end of it all I will help you discover the true meaning of love and peace that many strive their whole lives to obtain."

The old man picked up his cup of tea and looked up at Virgil.

"The choice is now in your hands my young friend...take your time and choose wisely"

The old man began to sip on his tea. Virgil stood

there in silence, wondering if he should actually trust in what the old man was saying.

"Take a risk..on myself you say? How do I know I can trust what you're saying to me?" asked Virgil.

The old man smiled and said "you can't...but that's why we call it a risk."

Virgil looked down at the cup of tea, and from the back of his mind he heard a silent whisper.

"Sit down Virgil" the whisper said.

Virgil turned around to look and see if anyone else was there, but there was no one else. With a sigh, Virgil sat down next to the old man, picked up the cup of tea and took a sip.

"Interesting...This is actually really good" said Virgil

"I told you it would be!" said the old man.

CHAPTER 2

THE TEMPLE

Two weeks had passed since Virgil accepted the old man's challenge. Still trying to put the pieces together of who the old man was, and how he knew so much about him. The old man and Virgil agreed to meet again on the last Sunday, of the month of February, at 6am. The old man had given Virgil three instructions to attempt before their next meeting. Virgil was to attempt to drink one gallon of water, sit in the sunlight for an hour and sit in complete darkness (without falling asleep) every single day. He was given until the end of the month to attempt these tasks, which to him seemed very simple...at first. He was unable to drink a gallon of water every day because of his juice addiction. The sun was just too hot for him to sit in for an hour a day and he could not sit in the dark without falling asleep ten minutes later. He was beginning to feel the old man was wasting his time just like the therapist.

The sun slowly began to rise on the last Saturday of the month, the day before Virgil was supposed to meet the old man. The light, from the sun, began to shine bright into Virgils room, slowly waking him. Virgil turned, grabbed his phone, checked his messages and began scrolling through his different social media accounts. Even though he just met the old man, who promised to help him through his struggles, he still felt as if his life was going nowhere. He slowly got out of the bed, put on some black joggers, with a white t-shirt and sat in the living room to play his video games.

Virgils cousin walked out of his room and into the living room.

"Video game and chill Saturday?" ask Cole.

"Yep, nothing else better to do my friend" said Virgil.

The two sat in the living room together, playing the game and enjoying the moment. Then Virgils phone began to buzz. Virgil grabbed his phone and saw that he had a messages from a random number.

Virgil checked the message from the random number, and it read "Put the game down, go outside and get some SUN!

Virgil threw the phone on the couch and looked outside of the living room patio window.

Cole looking confused "You okay bro?" he asked

Virgil turned and looked at Cole "...Yea, I'm good...just had a weird moment."

He turned and looked out the window, and there sitting at the patio door looking at him was none other than Kema. Virgil turned to Cole "Cole, come here and tell me what you see."

Cole got up and walked to the patio door.

"I see absolutely nothing bro" said Cole,

Virgil looked and Kema was still sitting there looking at him. She shook her head from side to side, not to alert anyone of her presence. Virgil sighed, turned around and gave his controller to

Cole.

"I'll be back" said Virgil.

Cole still looking confused "okay bro."

Virgil slightly opened the patio door, walked outside and closed it behind him.

He walked up to Kema and asked "Did the old man send you Kema?"

She meowed, turned, walked into the sunlight and laid down.

Virgil walked behind her and stood in the sunlight.

"Do we really have to do this now?" ask Virgil.

Kema turned, placed her paw on Virgils shoulder and meowed.

Virgil looked down "What? You like my shoes?" he asked?

Kema shook her head side to side and meowed again.

"Kema, I don't understand cat language. I'm a human...you're cat. Again...human...cat...you see the difference?" said Virgil.

As Virgil and Kema remained in the hot sunlight, the wind began to blow. Inside of the wind, the whisper of a womans voice came to Virgil.

"Take off your shoes" said the wind.

Virgil still being defiant asked, "no, why must I take my shoes off?! This makes no sense!"

Cole looked out of the patio window and saw that his cousin was yelling at the wind.

"I think my cousin is going crazy" said Cole.

The wind began to blow harder, as if it was trying to push Virgil into the air.

"Take off your shoes" the wind said again.

Virgil now panicking raised his hands into the air "Okay, okay! I'll do it!" he shouted.

Virgil quickly took his shoes and socks off. Placed them the side and placed his now bare feet into the warm green grass. He looked at Kema "Happy?" he asked.

Kema meowed and laid her head down. Virgil sat down next to Kema as the sunlight shined brighter onto both of them. About an hour and a half went by, and Virgil began to get thirsty. He looked at Kema "I'm going inside now; I gave you and the sun my time." Virgil stood up, grabbed his shoes and began to walk back into his apartment. As he reached the door he turned around and Kema, yet again, had vanished. He shook his head walked inside. His cousin looked at him, laughed and asked, "what was all that about bro?"

Virgil shook his head and began walking towards the kitchen.

"If I told you, you wouldn't believe me" said Virgil.

He walked into the kitchen, opened the fridge and grabbed a bottle of juice. As he began to open the bottle, he turned around and there standing on the kitchen table was Kema, glaring at him. Virgil looked down, into his hand, at the juice and back up at Kema.

"No" said Virgil.

Kema continued to glare at him.

"You already took me into that hot blazing sun, you're not taking my juice away!" said Virgil.

Cole leaned and look into the kitchen at Virgil.

"Who are you talking to bro?" asked Cole.

Virgil turned, looked at Cole and back at Kema.

"No one bro…just talking to myself" said Virgil.

He mouthed the word NO to Kema and began to motion the juice towards his mouth.

Kema leaped towards Virgil, he dropped his juice, closed his eye, reached out and shouted "Kema chill!"

Cole stood up and walked into the kitchen. There was juice everywhere and Virgil standing there as if he was waiting to catch something.

"You're acting really weird bro…and whose Kema?" said Cole.

Virgil opened his eyes and saw that there was no one but Cole and him in the kitchen.

Virgil looked at Cole and down at the juice on the floor.

"Too much sun, I'm just hallucinating. I just need some fresh water" said Virgil.

Virgil grabbed a towel and began cleaning up the juice. He then open the fridge, and grabbed the gallon of spring water on the bottom shelf.

He turned to Cole, with the water in hand and asked, "May I?"

Cole shrugged it and went back to the living room.

As the remainder of the day went by, Virgil did everything he could to drink an entire gallon of water. Night fall came and Virgil was in his room listening to some music, still trying to finish his gallon of water. Virgil slowly began to fall asleep and as his eyes began to close a furry friend began to walk onto his chest. Virgil let out a sigh, opened his eyes and saw Kema sitting on his chest.

"Kema, I've done everything the old man asked of me. What do you want now?" asked Virgil. Kema looked up at the ceiling and meowed towards the ceiling light. Virgil looked up at the light. "What? what's wrong with my light? You're always find something wrong" said Virgil. Kema walked off of Virgils chest, jumped on to the table next to the bedroom door, and jumped up at the light switch turning off the lights.

"...I really am starting to dislike you Kema" said

Virgil.

Kema jumped back up onto Virgils chest and laid down. Virgil continued to lay there in the dark. As the moon light began shining into Virgils room, he slowly began to fall asleep again. As his eye lids began to shut, and his breathing began to relax, a sudden chill came rising up to his spine. Virgil felt the presences of a hand touch his chest, and a final whisper "Remember me" went through his ears. Virgil opened his eyes and looked at Kema laying on his chest, leaned his head back and fell asleep.

PT.2

THE BODY AND THE MIND

It was 6am on Sunday morning and Virgil pulled up to the Jade Dragon ramen restaurant with Kema. Vigil walked up to the front door of the restaurant. On the front door there was a signed that read, "come to the cherry blossom tree and follow the path."

Virgil walked around the ramen restaurant to the cherry blossom tree.

Sitting under the tree, meditating, was an older black man. Virgil began to approach the old Asian man but before he got any closer Kema jumped in front of him and stopped him in his tracks as a sign to leave the man alone. Kema then lead Virgil to a trail on the far side of the tree and they both journeyed deep into the forest. The path was long and the deeper they went into the forest, the stranger it became. The trees began to look massive and the plants began to look strange but majestic. As if they were from another world. Virgil and Kema walked for what had seemed to be hours on this path. The path finally came to a stop, and in front of them was a beautiful bright blue lake. In the center was a wooden path, similar to a bridge, that led to what looked like a large size hut in the shape of a pyramid, which also looked as if it was made out of different stones and crystals. Surrounding the lake was the greenest grass one could ever imagine and from there were seven large trees around the lake, each with leaves of different colors. Virgil stood there gazing at the scene when he heard a familiar voice.

"Welcome to my home!" shouted the old man.

Virgil looked at the hut and saw the old man standing there.

"You live here?!" asked Virgil in a surprised voice.

The old man laughed and began walking towards him. Kema ran off to the left side of the lake, where she then climbed up one of the strange trees. The tree had emerald colored leaves, brighter than any other green tree in the forest. One of the leaves fell from the tree and floated over to Virgil. It landed right in front of him and began to shine brighter while in the suns ray of light. The old man walked up to Virgil and saw the leaf.

""Awwwe Anahata, always showing love to those who enter into the forest"

said the old man.

He picked up the leaf and placed it in his robe pocket.

"I'll be needing this sometime in the future" said the old man.

The old man looked at Virgil and greeted him again.

"How have the past two weeks been for you, my friend?"

"Terrible.." said Virgil.

The old man laughed and motioned his hand for

Virgil to follow him.

Virgil and the old man walked into the hut, and as Virgil entered, a sudden comforting chill surged through his body. It was as if all his worries and problems had been lifted. The old mans hut seemed like an exotic collectors' home. He had different stones and crystals on every corner of the hut. There were collections of books, articles, and manuscripts written in different languages. He had a table with a variety of candles, herbs, feathers, sea shells and statues. In the center of the hut was a medium sized hole, that connected itself to the lake water. Two small chairs were located next it and from the hole was a dim light fading in and out.

"You have a very...interesting place here" said Virgil.

"Thank you, it's the simple things that can make the spirit feel at peace" said the old man.

They both walked to the center of the hut to the two chairs and sat down.

"So, were you able to follow my three instruction?" asked the old man.

"So, about those..." said Virgil.

"Look, I did what I could. The sun was hot, the water tasteless and I was sleepy at night… I tried."

"Sounds like human excuses" said the old man.

"Excuses?! You wanted me to sit in the sun for an hour! Drink a gallon of water and sit in complete darkness without falling asleep!"

"Exactly, simple and easy instructions" said the old man.

"This is ridiculous…you're really wasting my time."

"Oh am I?" asked the old man.

"Yes you are…how is any of that supposed to help me?" asked Virgil.

The two sat in silence for a brief moment collecting their thoughts.

"Before you can begin any journey, whether it is to grow or heal, you have to understand your own capabilities" said the old man.

"Virgil, before you can begin any journey, whether it's with me or by yourself, you have to learn self-discipline."

"What does learning self-discipline have to do with any of this?" asked Virgil.

"Self-Discipline is the art of being able to overcome your weaknesses by controlling your feelings, thoughts, emotions, temptations and mind. When I gave you the three instructions, it was to see if you could have self-discipline. You failed of course, but you tried on the last day and succeeded. There is hope for you" said the old man.

Virgil nodded his head and understood what the old man was telling him.

"Do you mind if I ask you some questions?" asked Virgil

"Why of course not, now is the perfect time for you to ask your questions" said the old man.

"What was the purpose, other than self-disciple, of the three tasks? asked Virgil.

The old man sat up straight in his chair and cleared his throat.

"The task that dealt with you being in the sun and in the dark are very important. There are many reasons for this. One, you and me both, my friend are what many are called a melanated or eumelanated beings."

"Melanated Being…huh?" asked Virgil

"Yes indeed, let me explain. Melanin…is a chemical found in all living things. From bacteria, to plants, animals and even, more present, inside of the human body. Melanin gives our skin it's pigmentation, it regulates our body, boots our memory, helps us with aging, strengthens us mentally and spiritually and oh so much more. That, was the first reason."

Virgil looking confused, continues to follow along with the old man.

"My next reason is really going to blow your mind. Literally!" said the old man as he laughed.

"When we look on the top of the human head, we all have a brain. Within that brain we have all the lobes, that connect to the spinal cord, that then help the brain to function and all of that amazing science. What many people fail to mention, is that there is one part of the brain that goes unnoticed…Which part do you think that is?" asked the old man.

Virgil, confused, placed his hand on his head.

He began to massage his head as if he was dissecting his brain."

"Look, I was terrible in science okay. I barely paid attention" said Virgil.

The old man laughed again and pointed to the center of his forehead.

"Here" he said.

"In the center of our brain, there is a very small section for a very special organ. The ancients called this organ the third eye, or the master gland. It is very small, about the size of a kernel or corn but the shape of a pinecone. When this very small organ, comes into contact with the sun on a daily basis, your body, your mind and your spirit will begin to go through so many amazing changes.

Virgil, now even more confused than ever, just blankly stared at the old man in awe.

"Then, we have the sun" said the old man.

"One of the most powerful and amazing stars in the sky."

The old man stood up and looked at Virgil.

"Come with me" he said.

The old man walked outside of the hut and Virgil followed. They both stood in light of the sun. Feeling the heat coming down from the sky and onto their body.

"The sun, my dear boy, is the source of pure cosmic energy. The heat, the light, and even the sound of the sun can be very vital and beneficial to the human body. This is where life truly is my friend, in the sun. Feel it, embrace it, love it" said the old man.

As they both stood in the sunlight, the wind began to blow, the trees began to move side to side, and the water began to splash.

The old man turned and lead Virgil back into the hut. As they returned back to their seats, the old man grabbed a lit candle, a seashell and one of the herbs from a table in the hut. He brought them both back to his seat and began to light the herb with the candle. He closed his eyes and began to say a prayer to himself and whispered the word "Ase" after he had finished. He placed the shell into the water in the hole, with the herb on top of it. The old man sat back in his chair, closed his eyes, he breathed in very deeply through his nose and slowly released the air through his mouth.

"The task to embrace yourself in darkness, is just as important as going into the sun."

The old man pointed to the center of his forehead again.

"It all goes back to this small, amazing organ in our brain. This third eye, activates many things inside of us when in darkness. When in pure darkness, you can hear, feel, and sense things that are no typically there. The more you grow and train in this area, the more you will understand....Now take a deep breath with me Virgil."

Virgil sat up straight in his chair.

"Inhale through your nostrils deep....and exhale through your mouth ready?

INHALE!.......EXHALE" said the old man.

The both of them did this for approximately 10 mins and relaxed on the last breath.

After Virgils final breath, he leaned over to look in the water.

"Ahh that brings me to the water" said the old man.

Virgil looked up at him and back down at the water.

"Natural water is very important to our body. It cleanses, nourishes and hydrates our bodies…This task, and the others as well, will prepare you for what is to come."

Virgil looked up at the old man in confusion.

"What exactly is coming?" asked Virgil.

The old man sat back in his chair and looked at Virgil.

"Before I can share any true knowledge, teaching and guidance with you, you must first take responsibility and cleanse your temple."

"My temple?...meaning my body? Asked Virgil?

"Precisely" said the old man.

"What's wrong with my body?" asked Virgil.

The old man leaned over and looked into the water with Virgil.

"The body…is like the earth. Beautiful, Perfectly made, Self Healing, Protective, Nurturing and also very… secretive."

"Secretive?" asked Virgil.

"Yes indeed...You see, when we look at the earth and the body as one we see many similarities. When there is toxin, pollution, junk, waste and negative chemicals in both, neither one can operate to it's fullest capabilities...But...when we remove, detox and cleanse all of that negative energy... we begin to discover many different secrets that were hidden from us" said the old man.

"Interesting..." said Virgil.

"Interesting indeed...the earth is the pathway to the universe, just as the body is the pathway to the mind...look into the water Virgil."

Virgil leaned and looked into the water...but saw nothing but his reflection.

"I just see myself" said Virgil.

The old man looked down in the water and placed his hand on the surface.

"You only see yourself you say?...Interesting...By the end of this journey I am going to as you the same question...and if your answer is the same...I will reveal to you a secret lost and forgotten on this world that no other man knows."

"First a challenge, now a secret…sure why not?" said Virgil.

The old man smile and stood to his feet. At the entrance, there was a medium sized, older, bald, bearded man, with brown skin who had walked into the hut. It was the same man, who was meditating in front of the cherry blossom tree. The old man turned toward the entrance.

"Ahhh, Aynu my good friend, you've arrived just in time" said the old man.

Both of the older men walked up to each other, bowed and grabbed each other by the forearm to exchange greetings.

"I felt in my spirit, the time had come my friend" said Aynu.

Both of the men walked over to Virgil.

"Virgil, I want you to meet the man who will be assisting you on this journey.

This is Master Aynu, Aynu this is my new young apprentice, Virgil."

Aynu bowed before Virgil and extended his

hand. Virgil shook the mans hand and both the men let out a laugh.

"Much to learn this one has" said Aynu.

"Indeed, but he has high potential" said the old man.

Virgil let go Aynus hand and sat back down in confusion.

The two older men sat down next to him.

"Virgil, Aynu has agreed to train you and help you get your body into shape. While I educate you and guide you through this process."

Aynu turned and looked at Virgil

"My training is very difficult…many have attempted and failed. It takes discipline, dedication and most of all patience….Looking at you now, I see you lack all three… My son this process you're about to begin is not an easy one…are you sure this is something that YOU want?" asked Aynu.

Virgil looked at both men and let out a sigh.

"Look, I came here because this old man offered to help me through some of my life issues. He knows…too much about me and it intrigued me…

but all this other stuff, I didn't ask for this" said Virgil.

Aynu turned and looked at the old man and back at Virgil.

"Old man? Does he not know your name?!" Aynu asks the old man.

"We actually haven't gotten that far yet Aynu" said the old man.

"Nonsense! This is why the boy lacks confidence and is unsure. He has no idea of the man leading him on this path!"

Aynu turned towards Virgil.

"Young man… this is the Great Master Net.

Virgil looked up at the old man.

"Master Net?"

"Yes…Indeed" said Master Net.

"Master Net is wise, and very intune with not only the earth but the cosmos. If you're here and he has selected you to be an apprentice…I…would be more than honored" said Aynu.

Master Net let out a laugh and placed his hand

on Aynus shoulder.

"There's a reason why we're great friends Aynu."

Virgil stood up and looked at both of the masters.

"What are you two asking me to do?" asked Virgil.

Both men looked at each other, stood up and looked at Virgil.

"We're not asking you to do anything but follow your gut" said Master Net.

"When you listen to your gut, many times, that is your spirit or higher self, talking to you...It may seem risky or even farfetched, but I guarantee you, it's the best for you" said Aynu.

Virgil was hesitant and nervous and didn't know what to do or say. Could he actually trust these two old men to guide him and help him with his problems? What exactly did they know? And most of all, why him?

"Do it Virgil"

A strange voice spoke to Virgil deep in his mind.

"Do it…they mean no harm…and they will guide you to me" said the voice.

Virgil looked at the old men and with no more hesitation

"I'll do it" said Virgil.

Both of the men looked at each other and smiled.

"It has begun Master Net"

"Yes it has" said Master Net

Master Net walked over to one of his tables and began putting a collection of herbs in a bag.

"Virgil…your training with me will begin tomorrow morning at 4:30am infront of the cherry blossom tree" said Master Aynu.

"4:30am!!!" shouted Virgil.

"Precisely" said Master Aynu.

Virgil slapped his forehead and began to rethink all of his last decisions.

"Everyday, you will learn proper techniques to physically train the body. Every minute and day must count."

"What have I agreed to?" Virgil internally asked himself.

Master Net walked up to Virgil, handed him a bag, and a pamphlet.

"Master Aynu will help you train and discipline your temple…I will teach you and help you heal your temple. As I said before, the body is the pathway to the mind. Heal and discipline your body, and then you will be open to receive my knowledge" said Master Net.

Virgil looked down into the bag where there are other smaller bags inside.

"What exactly are these?" asks Virgil.

"What I have given you is a bag of four special herbs, in capsule and powder form, to jump start you off. Those herbs are Haritaki, Mucuna, Moringa The Miracle Tree, and a special combination known as the colon herb. Inside the pamphlet is information on each herb and instructions, that I designed myself, on how to take them and help the body reset itself. You must follow them exactly how it says. Understand?" asked Master Net.

Virgil had no other choice but to nod his head

and continue to listen.

"Perfect" said both the masters.

"From this day forward, you will no longer partake in the consumption of meat, dairy, or toxic substances" said Master Net.

"EXCUSE ME?!?!?" Shouted Virgil "You're taking my meat and cheese away!! Nope I'm drawing the line right there! Meat is good for you, there is research out there that proves it! What about protein? Iron? Uhhh zinc? And all the nutrients?! Nope Absolutely NOT.." said Virgil.

Both masters looked at each other and shrugged.

"Well I guess you aren't strong enough for this after all" said Master Aynu.

"I'm strong enough for anything!" stated Virgil! "It's just you're taking away something that I love."

"You wanted to know and accepted the way to fix your problems. These are the solutions. Either follow, or not" said Master Aynu.

Virgil turned and looked at Master Net

"Virgil...I would...the universe would never send you down a path you were not ready to handle.

You're here for a reason. It's up to you to make the decision...Before you can journey to peace, you have to become clean. Life is always changing, are you willing to learn to adapt?" asked Master Net.

From the front entrance, Kema walked into the hut. She walked over to Virgil and sits next to him. She looks up, gives him a meow and places a paw on his shoe.

"Kema, believes in you and she will be there with you every step. Just as we will" said Master Net.

"Gives us three months, and I guarantee you, you will change" said Master Aynu.

"Why three months?" asked Virgil.

"It takes three months, or ninety days to be exact, to reprogram what is known as the subconscious mind. Removing old habits and replacing them with new ones. If you follow our teachings and guidance, you will be ready for the next stage" said Master Net.

Virgil shook his head in disbelief.

"This is just, too much" said Virgil.

Master Net walked over to Virgil and placed his

hand on his shoulder.

"Go home and take Kema with you. We have given you enough information and guidance for the day. Ultimately the decision is yours and if this is what you want, Master Aynu will see you at sunrise.

Virgil let out a sigh and began walking towards the entrance.

As he walked outside, the light from the sun shined down onto him. The warm heat from the sun gave Virgil a sense of comfort. He walked towards the path along with Kema and began to head home. The two masters walked outside of the hut, watching Virgil leave the forest. Master Aynu turned towards Master Net.

"Do you think he'll make the right decision?" asked Master Aynu.

Master Net stood there in silence for a brief moment watching Virgil walk away.

It was 4:00am on Monday morning and Master Aynu sat in front of the cherry blossom tree, pouring himself a cup of tea. He reached into his rob and placed a small statue of a monkey onto the table in front of him. He took a sip of his tea and began to position himself for a quick mediation. As the time went by 4am turned into 4:25am. He sat patiently, still in meditation. The morning wind began to blow and cherry blossom tree began to softly sway left and right. The time had reached 4:30am and as Master Aynu began to come out of his meditation state, he saw standing off to the side was none other than Virgil. Virgil walked over to Master Aynu along with Kema, he bowed and sat down next to him.

"I didn't want to disturb" said Virgil.

Master Aynu greeted him with a head nod and extended his hand out to Virgil.

Virgil grabbed Aynu by his forearm and Aynu grinned.

"You learn quick" said Aynu

"I try" said Virgil "So, what is my first official lesson?" he asked.

Aynu grabbed his cup of tea and took a sip.

"Lesson number one, always start your morning with a warm cup of lemon and ginger tea" said Aynu.

He poured a cup of tea for Virgil and they both began their first day with a warm cup of tea.

CHAPTER 3

THE FOUNDATION

The morning sun began to rise in the east on the new beginning of June. The light from the sun began to shine upon the forest waking up the trees, plants and forest animals. Master Net was sitting outside of his hut, watching the sunrise and the forest come to life. Next to him, he had his favorite morning ginseng tea. He picked up his cup and added some crushed elderberry powder to it. He took a sip and with a sigh of peace afterwards he began his morning. He stood up and walked over to one of the strange trees found surrounding his hut. The tree was tall and covered with bright ruby leaves. One on the leaves fell and landed in front of

Master Net. He picked up the leaf and placed his hand onto the tree. He closed his eyes, took a deep breath and whispered to the tree.

"The time has come…wake up Muladhara."

The leaf, that was in the Masters hand, began to shine. As the Master removed his hand from the tree, the light from the leaf slowly faded and the leaf crumbled away. The Master turned and looked up at the rising sun.

"It's already been three months? Whew… time, is surely flying by….The real journey can now begin."

The Master smiled and began to walk towards the path leading out of the forest. As he walked on the path a new friend came and landed on his shoulder.

"Ahh, a red robin. Whose spirit dwells inside of you my friend?" asked Master Net.

The bird chirped, flew off in front of him and landed on the cherry blossom tree.

"Strange" said Master Net.

He looked and saw his friend Master Aynu

sitting under the tree meditating. He walked up and sat next time while drinking his tea.

"Aynu my friend, today marks the day of the beginning."

Aynu opened his eyes and looked at Master Net

"Indeed…the boy has been training his body for three months now. I believe he is ready."

"Where is Virgil by the way?" asked Master Net.

"Today is Sunday, the first of June. I gave him this day of from training so he could prepare his mind for his first lesson with you. Kema will bring him to you at noon."

Master Net nodded his head "Then, I shall go ahead and make the preparations. I've already spoken to Muladhara. She is ready to begin."

Aynu turned and looked at the cherry blossom tree. "That boy has shown great dedication these last three months. Even though his training with me will continue, nature's test is very…different compared to mine" said Aynu.

"Within nature lies the secrets to self and the universe. It only shows those answers that are worthy. The test are very difficult and they are like that for a reason. Only the strong and chosen can surpass" said Master Net.

Master Aynu turned and looked Master Net "Why this boy Master Net?"

"I beg your pardon?" asked Mater Net.

"Many have come, seeking your guidance. What makes this boy...this young man, so different? What life problems was he facing that were different from others?" asked Aynu.

Master Net took a sip of his tea and let out a sigh.

"This boy...this man... has the power to shift every mind and spirit on this planet. I know this because it is already written...I just have to wake him up" said Master Net.

The two Master's sat in silence for a brief moment. Master Aynu stood up and extended his hand to Master Net.

Master Net grabbed Master Aynu by the forearm and stood to his feet.

"If what you say is true Net...I will continue to

make sure the boy's body is strong enough, so his mind will be able to receive the knowledge you have."

"Thank you my friend" said Master Net.

Master Aynu began walking towards the Ramen restaurant and Master net turned and began walking on the path home. The wind began to blow and the voice from spirit of the forest came to Master Net.

"One year" the voice said.

Master Net stopped and looked up at the sky.

"He will be ready" and continued on the path.

Meanwhile, at his home, Virgil was outside laying on the grass enjoying the early morning breeze.

"Three months and those old guys have been able to get me outside like this? Never would have thought."

Virgil laughed as the light from the sun shone down upon him. Virgils cousin Cole walked up to him and placed a bottle of water next to him.

"Usually I'm the one up early in the mornings, what has gotten into you these last few months?" asked Cole.

Virgil grabbed the bottled of water and took. a sip.

"Just a different approach to life I guess" said Virgil.

Cole smirked and nodded his head

"Well, whatever approach this is, keep it up...You look healthy and happy man. I'm proud of you."

Virgil looked up at Cole happy to hear those word

"Thanks bro...That means a lot."

Cole turned and began walking back to the apartment. As he was walking back Kema passed by him and ran up to Virgil.

Cole, still unable to see Kema, felt a strong presence walk by him. He turned and looked back at Virgil but saw nothing.

"Weird" said Cole, and he returned inside the apartment.

Kema jumped onto Virigls chest surprising him.

"Kema it's not noon yet"

Kema had in her mouth, the bag of herbs Virgil had been taking for the last three months. Virgil looked and grabbed the bag.

"Oh, I forgot I am on a schedule."

Virgil reached into his bag and grabbed one of the capsule herbs.

"That old man was on to something when he gave me these. I haven't felt this good in...ever" he laughed.

Virgil took his daily herbs and stood to his feet. He began to embrace the light and heat from the sun while stretching his body.

"To think, I started off at 250 pounds, I'm almost down to 215 pounds. Look at me Kema...I look good!"

Kema looked up at Virgil and turned her back.

"There's always one hating on you" said Virgil

Virgil began to do his new morning routine that Master Aynu had been teaching him. Early morning yoga stretches to wake the body up. A 3-mile jog to get the heart pumping and blood flowing throughout the body. Finally, a series of cardio and strength building exercises to enhance the body.

"Master Aynu was definitely a pain, but I am grateful for what he has taught me" Virgil thought to himself.

Finally after his last workout, he returned to his apartment. He showered and began getting prepared for his meeting with Master Net. As Virgil began to leave his apartment, he turned and bumped into a woman.

"My bad, excuse me, I did not see you there" said Virgil

"Oh no, you're fine" she said, "I was just coming to introduce myself. I'm your new neighbor, Brya"

Brya was a short, dark brown woman. She had on a pair of dark red circular glasses, that matched her red tank top, along with light blue jean shorts and a pair of red low cut sneakers. She wore a small golden ankh necklace around her neck and her hair was beautifully, naturally, curled that fell to her shoulders.

Virgil was stuck and amazed at the same time.

"H….Hi, I'm Virgil"

Brya grinned and extended her hand to greet him.

Before Virgil could close his apartment door and greet her back, Cole opened the door.

"And I'm Cole, the roommate and cousin, how are you" Cole grabs Bryas' hand and greets her.

Brya began to laugh

"I'm good, nice to meet both of you"

Virgil looked and glared at Cole and thought to himself

"Did he really just do that?!?!" Virgil asked himself

Virgil looked back at Brya

"It's nice to meet you Brya, if you need anything just let us know" said Virgil

"Thank you, I appreciate that" said Brya

Virgil began walking towards his car as Brya and Cole began to talk.

Kema was waiting for Virgil on top of his car observing the situation.

Virgil opened the car door and sat down in the drivers seat. Kema hopped into his lapped and into the passengers' seat. He looked up at Cole still talking to Brya.

"Count your blessings Cole" said Virgil

He cranked his car and went on his was to meet Master Net.

PT. 2

ENTER MULADHARA

Virgil pulled up to Jade Dragon ramen restaurant and parked the car. Both he and Kema hopped out the car and began walking around towards the cherry blossom tree. Waiting for him was Master Aynu. Virgil walked up and bowed before Aynu and greeted him.

"Greetings Master Aynu"

Master Aynu greeted Virgil back with a bow and extended his hand for the greetings. After they greeted each other Aynu escorted Virgil and Kema to the path leading to Master Net's home. Master Aynu looked at Virgil

"Today marks the day for the beginning of your true journey...Today will not be easy. As my student, I send positive energy on your journey and wish you nothing but success."

"Thank you Master Aynu" said Virgil

"I will be waiting for your return with Master Net."

Virgil nodded and began walking with Kema on the path to Master Net.

Master Aynu sighed and looked up into the sky

"Mother Universe, he's in your hands now.

Virgil walked on the path until he arrived at Master Nets Hut. Master Net was standing outside waiting for Virgil to arrive with what seemed to be clothing in his hand.

Virgil walked up to Master Net while Kema ran off to the left side of the hut.

"Greetings Master Net, I suppose those are for me?" asked Virgil

"Indeed, go inside and change." said Master Net.

Master Net handed the clothing to Virgil, and

Virgil proceeded inside to change his clothing. The clothing he received was a black pair of baggy harem pants and a Black robe with seven colored circles on the back side. The colors consisted of, from top to bottom, purple, indigo, blue, green, yellow, orange and red. The same colors as the seven trees surrounding the outer area of Master Nets hut.

After changing clothes Virgil walked back outside to front of the hut where the master was seated waiting for him.

"Come, sit with me Virgil."

Virgil sat down next to the Master

"How are you feeling today Virgil?"

Virgil sat and thought for a minute on his response.

"I'm, okay. No complaints."

"That's good to hear" said the Master.

"How has life been since transitioning from no meat, no dairy, no processed foods and fasting?"

"It's still hard and going cold turkey really shocked my body at first. Training and learning with Master Aynu really helped.

"Have you been taking the herbs I gave you?"

"Yes sir" said Virgil with a head nod

"Good...Before we begin today's lesson. I will first explain the purpose of the herbs. Then I will introduce you to some very close friends of mine and finally we will begin the first lesson...Understand?"

"Yes sir" said Virgil

The old man reached in front of him and grabbed a pot. He reached in and pulled out four bags.

"Inside these bags are the herbs I gave you. The first herb was Haritaki."

"Yea the pamphlet, you gave me, said it was to help with my overall body health" said Virgil

"Exactly, it is found in the India and the Southern part of Asia. This herb is very powerful when used correctly. It even can give the brain an increase in oxygen allowing for more brain activity."

The Master handed the bag of Haritaki to Virgil.

"Next we have Mucuna Pruriens, another herb

found in Asia as well as Africa."

"Yea, this one was supposed to help me with my motivation" said Virgil

"Correct, I see you've been reading. Mucuna, also known as velvet, beans, has high levels of dopamine. A compound found in the human body. Just like Haritaki this herb can help your overall brain function and must be taken properly."

Master Net handed the bag of Mucuna to Virgil.

"Now we have Moringa also known as the miracle leaf. This herb is located in the Himalayans of India and Pakistan. This herb is rich in many vitamins, nutrients, proteins, antioxidants and many more. It has been known to cure many diseases and it tastes great when cooked with foods."

The Master handed the bag of Moringa to Virgil.

"Finally, we have a special mixture of herbs that I mixed into these vegetable capsules, that assist with cleaning your colon. Now if you read the pamphlet like I told you too, you were to take the colon cleanse herb for ten days before doing anything else, correct?"

"That's correct...I felt terrible" said Virgil

"Great, that means it works! This is one the foundations and beginnings of cleaning the body. Since humans tend to eat a lot of toxic and unhealthy food, it weakens our body. The colon cleanse is an ancient method to cleanse the system of toxins allowing the body to maintain optimum health. Now you won't be needing another one of these. We're on to better."

The master placed the last herb back in the pot and stood to his feet.

"Come with me Virgil and place your herbs in the side pocket of your robe...It's time I introduce you to some very special friends of mine."

Virgil stood up to his feet and followed the master.

They began to walk to the front of the lake where they could see their entire surroundings.

As Virgil turned to look at the forest, he observed the seven strange trees as they began to glow and shine. The animals of the forest began to leave from the area. The clouds in the sky began to vanish, and the sun's light began to shine brighter than it ever had.

"Virgil…I want to introduce you to the seven sacred guardians of this forest. The Seven Chakras of Knowledge and Spirit.

Virgil eyes began to widen as the forest began to become alive. A leaf from each tree made its way to Virgil and landed right in front of him.

"The seven chakras of knowledge and spirit?" asked Virgil.

"Indeed…each sacred tree represents an energy stored within us. They have been waiting and watching you for a very long time Virgil…allow me to introduce you."

The leaves, from each tree that landed on the ground raised up into the hands of Master Net.

"First, we have Muladhara, the ruby root chakra. She represents foundation and her energy will bond you with the earth and grounding yourself in her soil" The Master handed the ruby leaf to Virgil.

"You hold on to her" said Master Net

Virgil took the leaf

"Next we have Svadhishthana, I just call her Hana. She is the orange sacral chakra. She represents creation and her energy will flow in you like a stream of water, Feeding and cleansing your soul with cosmic water... Then we have Manipura, the bright yellow solar chakra. Manipura will test your power and confidence, if you fail her test her solar flames can and will engulf you."

The Master released both the orange and yellow leaves into the wind.

"Now, we have a very familiar friend who greeted you the first time you stepped into the forest."

Master Net pulled out the emerald green leaf.

"Virgil meet Anahata, the emerald heart chakra."

The wind among the forest began to increase. Bright emerald leaves began to swirl around Virgil and Master Net.

"She's excited I see" said Master Net.

The wind slowed down and the leaves, that were engulfed within, slowly fell to ground.

"Anahata will dive deep into your emotions…your past and present life. With her power, she will assist with answering many questions and revealing light in the darkness."

Master Net turned and handed Virgil the emerald leaf.

"She precisely wants you to hold on her leaf throughout this entire process."

Virgil looked at the bright emerald leaf and deep within the leaf it looked as if there was a tiny white sphere floating around inside. Virgil brought the leaf closer to his eyes and what he saw were tiny white orbs floating inside the leaf.

"Ummmm, Master Net…What are these tiny orbs?" asked Virgil.

Master Net looked at the leaf and say the tiny little orbs floating inside.

"Those are tiny energy particles. They are what connect Anahata and the other trees to what we call the Akashic Realm" said Master Net.

Virgil continued to stare into the leaf as if he was beginning to become mesmerized by the white spheres. Master Net placed his hand over the leaf to bring Virgil back to the present moment.

"If you begin to look to deep, you'll find answers you're not ready to know or comprehend so…place Anahata in your robe pocket until it's time."

Virgil softly placed the leaf in his pocket and took a deep breath. Master Net nodded his head, pulled out the last three leaves and lead Virgil to the final three trees.

"Next we have Vishuddha, the blue throat chakra. This tree will help to fill that empty space inside of you with confidence to take control of your life. It will help you to express yourself and communicate with all things in life."

Virgil looked up at the blue tree, and as he started to gaze at it, the leaves on the blue tree began to pulse.

"She's speaking to you Virgil" said Master Net.

"She is?" asked Virgil

Master Net nodded "Indeed she is, you are not yet able to hear her, but she greets you and says to prepare yourself meet the final two trees. They are not to be taken lightly."

Virgil look back at the tree and he bowed before it

"Thank you" said Virgil

Master Net began to walk towards the final two trees who were rooted right next to one another. As they approached the trees, the light of the sun began to intensify. The light gave of an energy so intense that Virgil stopped walking towards the two tree's and stood in one place. It was as if the energy had paralyzed his body to the point where his body would no longer respond to him. Master Net stopped and turned around to look at Virgil.

"Virgil, what's the problem?"

Virgil didn't speak, he couldn't something had taken over his entire body.

Virgil slowly moved his eyes and looked at Master Net. He couldn't speak, he couldn't move. He was stuck in the sun's energy, paralyzed.

"Help me Master Net, I can't move my body" Virgil said to himself.

As Virgil stared at Master Net, a giant gust of wind came into the forest. Dark clouds began to form in the sky, but they did not block the suns light on Virgil or the last two trees. As the wind blew harder, Master Net vanished within the gust of wind.

"Master Net! Where did you go?!" Virgil panickily said to himself.

The wind engulfing Virgil slowed down and when it calmed down, the Master was gone. The only thing Virgil could see, where the final two trees.

"There's no one else here Virgil...only you and us" said a strange voice.

"Who...what was that?" said Virgil to himself.

"You may move now, we have granted you your body within this realm" said another strange voice.

Virgil began to slowly move his arms, then his legs and he looked around searching for Master Net.

"Who's there?! Where's Master Net?" Shouted Virgil.

"Your Master is not here. Only you and us" said both of the voices.

Before Virgil could ask another question, the light from the sun slowly began to direct its light only on Virgil. From the corner of Virgils eye, he saw that the last two trees began to shine bright. One had leaves with a calm light indigo color and the other had leaves with a dark purple color. Virgil turned towards the trees and began to walk towards them.

"Cease your movement" said the voices.

Virgil stopped in his placed and looked up at the trees.

As Virgil gazed at the trees, suddenly before his eyes, two orbs came out of both trees and floated towards Virgil. The orbs then began to shift into figures, that of a human form and began walking towards him. Virgil eyes open wide and he fell to the ground. He began to slowly back away from the figures as they approached him.

"CEASE YOUR MOVEMENT!" commanded the voices.

Virgil stopped moving and gazed upon the figures. The first figure to approach Virgil was the light calm indigo figure.

"Stand before me" said the figure.

Virgil slowly stood to his feet as the figure

commanded.

"Well done...you're learning sleeping spirit...My name is Ajna, the tree of cosmic insight. Unlike my sisters, I will not be so kind and easy on you. For my power is not something to be taken lightly. You are not even ready to see any of my sisters true form...but, there is a reason you're here."

Virgil did not speak but he bowed before the spirit showing respect towards her.

Ajna turned and began to return back to her tree. She looked at the figure she was standing next to.

"He's not ready sister, let us return" said Ajna.

Ajna returned to her tree while the other continued to stand in front of Virgil.

"Come to me Virgil" said the figure.

Virgil walked towards the figure as requested.

The spirit raised its right arm towards Virgil and extended its hand.

Virgil looked at the figure and began to raise his hand to grab the figures hand.

The two grabbed each other's hands and a sudden feeling of warmth and electricity raised from Virgils spine all the way to his neck.

"Interesting…I will free you my sleeping serpent" said the figure.

"Sleeping serpent?" asked Virgil

The figure let go of Virgils hand and began walking towards the tree it came from.

"Wait" said Virgil

The figure turned around and looked at Virgil.

"You are not yet worthy young spirit, but when the time comes…I Sahasrara will free you from this physical world and guide you home."

The figure turned and went back into the tree.

Virgil stood there gazing at both the trees as the light from them both began to fade. The dark clouds began to disappear, and the light of the sun began to cover the forest again.

"Virgil…Virgil!"

Virgil snapped out of his gaze to find Master Net standing in front of him.

"What…" Virgil began looking around and saw that everything was back to normal.

"You've been standing there for some minutes …everything alright?"

Virgil looked in front of him and saw Master Net standing next to both trees.

"Come Virgil, no time to just stand and gaze"

As Virgil began to slowly walk towards the trees, he felt a force, of some sort, pushing him back every step that he took.

"You are unworthy" said a voice in the air.

Master Net walked towards Virgil when he noticed he was struggling to walk towards the trees.

"What's the problem Virgil?"

Virgil, breathing heavily now, looked up at Master Net.

"I…I'm unworthy…they won't, allow me to come any closer" said Virgil

Master Net, with a look of confusion, turned and looked at the trees.

"Wait here Virgil"

Master Net walked towards the trees, sat in front of them and placed a hand on each tree.

"Ajna, Sahasrara…I honor and respect thee. I ask that you explain through me, the purpose of testing my apprentice this early."

Virgil looked up at Master Net and saw that he had begun to meditate. Kema, who had been sleeping, walked over to Virgil and placed a paw on his foot. Virgil still breathing heavy looked down at Kema "what are you doing Kema?" A tingly electrical feeling began to work it's way up from Virgils foot to the top of his head. As the small electrical feeling began to surge through Virgils body, he looked up at Master Net and saw a powerful white and indigio aura surrounding him.

"What the…Master Net…you're one of them?" said Virgil.

The aura from Master Net began to calm down and return back into his body. Master Net opened his eyes and looked at Virgil. He stood to his feet and walked over to him. Kema walked up to both of the trees and sat in the middle of them.

"Well…you were right. They see you as unworthy

to approach them" said Master Net.

"But why?" asked Virgil

Master Net took a deep breath and began walking back towards the front of the forest where the sacred trees began.

"Come, your inner work training starts now" said Master Net.

Virgil, now silent, began to follow Master Net to the first sacred tree of the forest, Muladhara. As they approach the tree, Master Net turned and stopped Virgil.

"Before we begin the first test I, as your Master, must warn you Virgil. These tests will not be easy. They will test you mentally, emotionally, physically and most of all spiritually. Everything you've ever been through in your life, whether good or bad will come to light. Do not fear it or run from it. All the answers you were searching for at your therapist, will be given to you on this journey...do you understand?"

Virgil nodded his head and looked at Muladhara.

"She's waiting for you" said Master Net, "But before you begin the test, I must teach you how to center yourself, control your breathing and relax your mind."

"You mean meditate" asked Virgil.

"Precisely" said Master Net

"But it is deeper than just meditating. You are learning what is known as breathwork. Control the breath and it will allow your mind and body to relax. By doing this, you can then receive the information from the trees, the universe and the cosmos."

"You keep saying information, what information? And where is exactly is this information coming from?" asked Virgil

"Take out that ruby leaf from within your robe pocket" said Master Net.

Virgil reached into his pocket and took out the leaf.

"Now look within it, just as you did when you looked into the emerald leaf" said Master Net

Virgil looked into the leaf and saw the same tiny white orbs floating inside.

"Those tiny white orbs of energy give you

information. Those orbs are connected to a sacred realm called the Akashic Records."

"And what exactly is the Akashic Record realm?" asked Virgil.

"Hmmmm, that is question that you must find the answer too"

"Why is that?" asked Virgil

Master Net grabbed one of the ruby leaves off of one of Muladhara's branches.

"If I told you what it really was…you wouldn't believe me" said Master Net with a grin.

"But that will come in due time, right now we must focus on the present and the task at hand. The foundation of your journey, which all begins with Muladhara. When approaching a sacred chakra, you want to approach with respect because nature and energy can sense a negative being. Now sit right in front of Muladhara facing her."

Virgil walked up and sat as instructed.

"Now, in order to approach the Muladhara, you have to ground yourself in the earth."

"Ground myself?" asked Virgil

"Indeed, when we ground ourselves, we connect with the earth. We feel the dirt, the soil, the grass. It's as if we are allowing our spirit to connect with the spirit of the earth."

"Uhhhh, huh" said Virgil. "And how exactly do I go about doing this?"

Master Net walked over and placed his hand on to the tree.

"Grounding and establishing a relationship are a process…Over the past two months, while you were training your body with Master Aynu, you trained with me in the art of meditating and breathing. Now it's time to put that training to…"

"Master?"

Virgil stood to his feet and walked over to Master Net, who was now in a frozen state. "I appreciate what he was doing but we do not have time for all of that talking" said a woman's voice from behind him.

Virgil turned around to surprisingly find a familiar face. It was his new neighbor, Brya.

"Brya? Wha…What are you doing here? And how are you doing this??"

"Ha!" laughed Brya, "To you in your human form I'm Brya, but in this realm…"

A burst of bright red light and energy began to surface from Brya. The earth beneath Virgil's feet began to move. The ruby tree behind him began to glow.

"In this realm…I am Muladhara, and you shall address me as such."

Virgil, now confused, was trying to find the words but couldn't.

"You're trying to figure out why I approached you earlier today, correct?" asked Muladhara.

Virgil nodded his head.

"As your first teacher I wanted to meet you myself. My sisters despise the physical world, but I tend to enjoy it. I wanted to see the kind of man you were before I allowed you to become my student. Your Master was more than happy to go along with this plan but that's in the past now"

Muladhara began walking towards Virgil and her tree.

"As the root chakra, I am responsible for

teaching you how to become more secure, stable, full of health, energy and vitality before proceeding to my other sisters. In order to do this, you must become one with my energy."

"Ummmm, okay" said Virgil

"Stop doubting yourself Virgil.." said Muladhara.

"Excuse me?"

Muladhara walked up towards Virgil and held her hand up.

"May I?" she asked

"Uhhh, sure?" Virgil responded

"You're doing it again" she said.

Muladhara placed her hand onto Virgils forehead and warm feeling began to transfer from her hand to his head. Virgil slowly began to fall to his knees and his eyes began to close.

"Relax your mind and let go" said Muladhara.

Virgil began to feel a sense of relaxation through his whole body. As if the world around him didn't exist anymore and he was one with himself.

"Virgil…." A soft voice called out.

"Virgillll…" the voice called out again.

"VIRGIL!!!"

Virgil opened his eyes, to find himself in a small room laying on top of a small bed. The room seemed very familiar, as if he had been there before. There were posters of superhero's, anime shows and cartoons on the wall. The was a small old tv on top of a dresser connected to an old videogame console. The room seemed to be the room of a boy.

"Virgil!! Get up here now!!" shouted the voice again.

"I'm coming, I'm coming" said the voice of a small voice.

Virgil got up out of the bed and walked over to the bedroom door entrance. He peeked his head outside and could not believe what he saw… It was him, when he was 7 years old, and his mother standing in their old living room.

"This isn't happening" said Virgil

"This is very much happening" said Muladhara from behind him.

Virgil turned around and saw Muladhara siting

on the bed reading what seemed to be an old manga book.

"Humans are such creative beings. They only seemed to scratch the surface when it comes powers and tapping into unknown energy" said Muladhara.

"Where...Why are we here?!" whispered Virgil.

Muladhara lowered the manga book "you're being very rude Virgil. Can't you see I'm enjoying one of your childhood books. It's very interesting so quiet please. You have other things to pay attention to then me" said Muladhara as she raised the book and pointed at the bedroom door.

"This is unacceptable young man! Do you have anything to say about this?" said the voice of a woman.

"I remember this day" said Virgil "This is when...when I got into a fight at school. Some of the kids wouldn't leave me alone...They wouldn't stop making fun of me, because I was a big kid, I dressed differently, and I talked different...I got so angry that I snapped and lost control. Ended up fighting all of them and getting kicked out of school...My parents were so angry with me but they didn't understand...I felt so alone and like an outcast with those kids and for them to always make fun of me, when I just wanted to make friends...It hurt...It hurt really bad..."

Tears began to slowly fall from Virgils face.

"It hurt the most...because my parents just wouldn't understand me and why I was so angry...I just wanted to make friends... and no one liked me..."

Muladhara lowered the manga book, and walked over towards Virgil.

She wrapped her arms around him from behind and comforted him.

"This...is the first step in growth Virgil. Tackling things in your past that caused you so much trauma, anger, and pain. This was one of the times where your energy, as a child, was very low and I'm here to tell you, it's time to let the hurt, from this moment, go."

Virgil turned around and looked at Muladhara.

"Why, did you bring me here?" asked Virgil

"I didn't, you did" said Muladhara "Well not

necessarily you but your subconscious did."

"My subconscious?" asked Virgil

"Indeed, your subconscious mind contains a lot of information on you. Even information that you probably didn't know. It even contains memories that defined who you are today."

Virgil turned and walked back towards the door and peeked over to watch his past memory unfold.

"Dwelling on the past gets you no where Virgil…Only when you have taken the time to learn from it and let it go, can you truly understand growth…"

As Virgil watched his younger self cry he knew that what Muladhara was saying was right. Muladhara walked up behind Virgil and placed a hand on his back. The warm energy feel began to flow from his spine to center of his head and with a few blinks, Virgil was back in front of Muladharas tree. Virgil turned and sat on the ground and looked at the lake water, reflecting on his past.

"I see Muladhara wasted no time in showing you her power" said Master Net walking up behind Virgil.

Virgil continued to sit in silence staring at the lake.

"If this process is going to be too much for you Virgil, I can definitely make arrangements for you to return back to your therapist"

Virgil continued to sit in silence, not purposely ignoring his Master, but just could not find the right words to respond.

"I think…I think I'll take that offer. Going to see the therapist. I'm not stopping this process, but I believe this helped me to want to open up on somethings" said Virgil

Master Net nodded his head and walked over to sit next to Virgil.

"I have so much to teach you Virgil, so many things I want to educate and share with you. I know if we continue on this path, you will learn so much from not only me but yourself as well."

As the Master Net and Virgil sat down watching the suns light reflecting off of the lakes water, Master Aynu appeared at the front of the forest and began walking towards them.

"So, how did everything go?" asked Aynu

"It went...well" said Master Net "The seven chakras have been waiting for this moment so they had to make their introductions very...interesting."

Virgil stood to his feet and looked at both the Master's.

"I'm about to go home. I need a break from today."

"Indeed" said both the Masters.

Virgil began walking off with Kema, who had strangely reappeared, followed behind him.

"Virgil!" shouted Master Aynu "Tomorrow morning...be here."

As Virgil continued to walk off he lifted a thumb into the air as a sign of understanding.

The master's watched as he continued to walk off.

"He's seen a lot in such a short amount of time" said Master Aynu.

"The fact that he can see and feel everything that has happens proves that my theory of him is correct" said Master Net.

"And that is?" asked Master Aynu

Master Net looked up into the sky as the sun slowly began lower from the sky.

"He's very special and he just doesn't know how important he is to the future of this world" said Master Net.

Master Net walked towards his hut along with Master Aynu.

"You know Net, the ancestors are watching this process. What do they say about all of this?"

Master Net began to laugh

"What do they say you ask? They're the ones pushing for all of this to fall into place!"

"Is that so?" asked Aynu

"It is….Aynu my friend, that young man is a very important piece to puzzle that has been forming for the last two thousand plus years…He is more important thank you think" said Net

Master Net walked into the hut, grabbed two small cups and a hot tea pot.

"You my friend, need a cup of this reishi and

camomille tea" said Net.

The two sat outside of the hut and began to drink their tea.

"The journey has just begun Aynu...the world is about to experience a major shift in the coming months and it starts with him... We must do our part like instructed."

Aynu nodded his head and continued sipping his tea.

The two Master's sat outside as the night sky began to approach, meanwhile Virgil had arrived home reflecting on his entire day. The memory of him as a little boy would not leave his head. Over and over it continued to play out. It seemed there was no end. Until there was a knock at the front door of his apartment. Virgil stood up and walked over to the door and answered.

As he open the door he saw that it was, yet again, Brya or was it Muladhara.

"Mula.."

"Ahhh, stop right there" said Brya "I told you, in this world outside the forest, I'm Brya. Don't forget that!" said Brya as she thumbed him on the forehead.

"Here, I brought you this" In her hand was a red flower, a tiny crystal and a hot cup of tea.

"You...you didn't have to" said Virgil.

"LISTEN I KNOW WHAT I DO AND DO NOT HAVE TO DO!! NOW TAKE THIS TEA AND THIS RED LOTUS FLOWER AND ZIP IT! Said Brya.

Virgil, a little scared took both of the items "Yes ma'am"

With a smile on her face "Good, now drink up. It's a tea used back in my time called Blue Lotus. Get use to it because of all my sisters use this tea. It has a strong taste to it so I did a blend of strawberries to help with the taste."

Virgil to a sip of the tea and even with the added strawberries it was still very bitter.

"It's drinkable" said Virgil

"Don't push it" said Brya "Oh also, that is a red lotus flower and a red jasper crystal. Very strong items and will help you in this process of connecting with your inner root chakra. Sit the flower close to you at night and always carry that stone with you. Trust me" said Brya.

"Thank you, I really appreciate the gifts" said Virgil

"Now go get some rest, I'll be waiting for you tomorrow. We're going to spend the next few weeks getting to know each other very well."

Virgil nodded his head, Brya turned and walked off. Virgil closed the door and walked to his room. He placed the red jasper and red lotus flower by his bed, while he continued to sip on the tea. As Virgil laid their on his bed, his eyes began to get heavy and sleeping effects of the tea began to set in. Virgil placed the cup of tea to the side and ventured off to bed, where he feel into a deep sleep. While in this state of sleep Virgil found himself in a void of darkness. A darkness that didn't seem frightening but wasn't comfortable either. The sound of someone crying echoed throughout the darkness.

"Hello…who's there?" asked Virgil

The crying continued but seemed to get closer and closer.

"Who's there?!" shouted Virgil.

"Why don't they like me?" said the voice. "Why won't they listen to me?"

Virgil turned around and looked down to see what happened to be the little version of himself on the ground crying.

"Why don't my parents listen to me?! I'm not violent, I'm not emotional...I'm just angry" said the boy.

Virgil slowly sat down in front of the boy and looked at him in concern.

"Why are you angry little guy?" he asked.

The boy looked up at him in tears.

"Because, no one likes me. I tried making friends, and they just keep making fun of me. I tried showing them that I was cool like them but it wasn't good enough. They laugh and laughed and I lost control. My parent's don't understand...they won't listen to me or understand me" said the boy.

The boy lowered his head and continued to cry.

Virgil moved closer to the boy and put his hand on his head.

"Hey kid, there's nothing wrong with you" said

Virgil

The boy looked up at him in confusion "Yes there is, if there wasn't anything wrong, I would have friends! My parent's wouldn't treat me like I didn't matter!"

Virgil shook his head "You got it all wrong man" said Virgil. "Those kids that don't want to be your friend, you don't need them. It's cool to be different and be the black sheep. You're special and fine just the way you are. Your parents? Yeah it's messed up how they treated you in some situations, but hey they're parents right?"

The little boy nodded his head, "I just want some one to care and love me for me...see me for who I am."

Virgil looked down at the boy "I love you little man" said Virgil.

The boy looked up at him "you do?" he asked "Why?".

Virgil nodded "Yea...because you're me, and I'm you. If no one else in this whole world loves you, I love you kid...No, I love you Virgil."

The boy looked up and smile "I've waited a long

time for you to say that" said the boy

He stood up and hugged Virgil. At that moment nothing else really mattered, except two beings both past and present finally accepting one another.

As Virgil laid there still in his deep sleep, outside his window sat Kema, watching over him along with another spiritual figure. This figure, however, was different from the others that Virgil met at the forest. It didn't want to test him or challenge him but simply watch him, as if it had been watching him for a very long time now.

The crescent moon creeped over the clouds and the figure vanished, knowing that it's time to meet Virgil was coming very soon.

PART 2

CHAPTER 4

THE FIRST TEST

"I now call this meeting to order"

Deep inside of the living universe, there is a realm of high spiritual and cosmic energy. Only those who have gained the knowledge and proven themselves worthy through the test of life and spirit may enter. This place is known as the Akashic Records. Inside this realm lies all the answers to the past, present, the future, the beginning and the end which is always going to be the beginning. Here in this realm, spirits and entities gather amongst one another sharing knowledge, experience and energy.

Here in this realm there is a sacred area, specially made for the seven chakras, known as the cosmic tree where the sisters come together to meet and discuss events of the future.

"Sister's, we come today to discuss the process and next steps of the apprentice of Master Net known as Virgil...Muladhara, come" said Ajna.

Muladhara was standing off to the side looking out at all of the spirits wandering the records.

"Muladhara!" said Ajna.

Muladhara slowly turned and looked at her sister.

"Come and speak on behalf of Nets student" said Ajna.

Muladhara walked towards her sister and stood in front of a bright red tree, filled with what seemed to be dust and particles from the cosmos.

"...For the past 3 months, I have worked, trained with Master Nets apprentice on unlocking his root chakra. He has shown much growth, and his root chakra has begun to flourish"

Five of the six sisters nodded their head in

agreeance, while Ajna sat still.

"I believe he is ready for the next test" said Muladhara.

"Svadhishthana…how do you feel about this sister?" asked Ajna

"I'm more than ready to see what this…growing spirit has to offer" said Svadhishthana.

Ajna looked at Sahasrara and they locked eyes.

"Is there a problem sister's?" asked Muladhara.

"Actually, we have a suggestion to bring to the sister's" said Sahasrara

The chakra sister's looked at one another in confusion. Ajna walked to the front next to Muladhara.

"We would like to increase the chakra awakening test difficulty" said Ajna

"Increase the test difficulty?!" shouted the sister's.

"Indeed" said Sahasrara "But it is not of our own request"

"Then who?" asked Muladhara

Sahasrara turned and walked towards Muladhara

"Now Muladhara, you know as the crown chakra there are certain things, I cannot reveal to you at this moment. I ask that you trust my...our suggestion."

Muladhara shook her head.

"Oh, what's wrong sister? You've been dwelling among the earth spirit's and gotten soft haven't you?" said Ajna.

A burst of red energy sparked from Muladhara.

"SILENCE AJNA!" said Muladhara

Ajna stood there with a grin on her face

"They don't call me the third eye chakra for no reason sister, I see right through you" said Ajna with a burst of indigo light energy coming from her.

The two sisters stood facing each other while the others watch.

"ENOUGH!!!" shouted Sahasrara.

"You both know that is not allowed in this realm... we NEVER bring that energy to the

Akashic Records! DO YOU UNDERSTAND!?! Shouted Sahasrara.

Both the sisters calmed their energy down.

"Yes sister" they both said.

"Good, now excuse yourselves" said Sahasrara.

Muladhara and Ajna looked each other in the eyes before walking out of the cosmic tree.

"Muladhara" said Sahasrara

Muladhara turned around and looked at her before walking out.

"Return back to Gaia and continue your training with Virgil. He has indeed grown, and I give you credit for that. Let Master Net know his next phase will start soon...very soon."

Muladhara nodded and exited the Akashic Records.

Sahasrara and the remaining sisters continued their meeting.

"Now, on to real business sisters" said Sahasrara

"I have met with an ancient ancestor of Gaia...there is a strong ancient energy returning back into the cosmos, and we have much work that needs to be done before it arrives."

Manipura, Svadhishthana and Vishuddha looked at one another.

"ancient energy?" asked Manipura.

"Indeed…" said Sahasrara

"So, is this the reason for wanting to increase the awakening trails?" asked Vishuddha

"Yes…the ancient ancestor is asking us to challenge Virgil and push him closer to full awakening. Once we've done our part, Master Net will fulfill his" said Sahasrara.

"Sister…what of Anahata? She is not present amongst us. Shouldn't she too be here?" said Manipura

All the sister's nodded.

"Anahata is already fulfilling her duty Manipura, once you three have done your part with Virgil she and Ajna will continue the rest" said Sahasrara.

"Understood sister" said the three-chakra sister's

"Now, there is work to be done. Go to Gaia and prepare yourselves. You all have one month to assist Virgil with unlocking his sacral, solar, and throat chakra" said Sahasrara.

"Yes sister" said the three sisters.

As the three sisters left the Akashic Records, Sahasrara stayed behind at the cosmic tree. She turned to the tree and walked towards it placing her hand onto the tree.

"I see it didn't take you long to arrive here?" said Sahasrara.

Standing a couple of feet behind her was a white light humanoid figure of energy. It walked up closer behind her and sat down in a meditative pose.

"Come Sahasrara, sit with me" said the figure.

Sahasrara turned towards the figure and sat down in front of it.

"How did your sister's take the proposal?" asked the figure.

"They were hesitant...but they are going forward with it" said Sahasrara

"Good, everything is coming together" said the

figure as it nodded.

"You haven't given me much knowledge of your intentions with this human boy" said Sahasrara

The figure reached its hand out towards the tree and a small wave of light energy flowed to her hand. The energy surged throughout the figure and it released it into Sahasrara. As the energy made its way throughout her, she began to receive visions of the future. Everything was beginning to make since.

"You being the crown chakra and the queen of the others, I would of expect you to have known these events already Sahasrara" said the figure

"I have known but you giving me the vision enhanced my knowledge on this. Unlike my sister's I have many things in the cosmos to attend to…but this…I will give it more of my attention now" said Sahasrara

The figure nodded "if the boy fails to awaken the kundalini serpent stored inside of him, we will have no choice but to wait another three thousand years for an awakening" said the figure.

"The are many humans already awakened on Gaia, why is this boy important?" ask Sahasrara

The figure smiled and began to stand up.

"The boy is a major piece of this giant cosmic puzzle. Master Net knows this, and all of the ancestors of Gaia know this. This is why we have watched him since he was born on Gaia. His awakening will set off a chain reaction... awakening other beings who will also play a part in this universal puzzle" said the figure.

The figure began walking towards the cosmic tree

"I am returning back to my realm, we will meet again once the boy has unlocked his sacral, solar, heart and throat chakras" said the figure

"Understood, may the cosmos and the energy of the universe be among on you" said Sahasrara

"Asé" said the figure as it light body began to enter into the cosmic tree.

Sahasrara stood up and looked into the cosmic sky

"The things we do just to have peace...I shall return to Gaia the day that peace returns."

PT. 2

UNLOCKING THE ROOT

"Breathe...... just breathe. Allow the prana to fill your lungs and stomach, as you visualize the energy at the base of your spine opening up like a red lotus flower....... Now awaken Virgil" said Master Net.

Virgil and Master Net were sitting under a tree deep in the sacred forest. Virgil had been learning a new breathwork technique taught to him by Master Aynu and was combining it with Master Net's meditation.

"How did I do this time?" asked Virgil

"You are definitely improving; I am very

impressed" said Master Net

The two stood to their feet and began to stretch.

"How's your training going with Muladhara?" asked Master Net

"Whew! It's been tough these last two months. Since May it has been nonstop and here we are in August. She is no joke when it comes to grounding and connecting to her chakra. I literally have spent my entire summer with her" said Virgil

Master Net began to laugh "this is why it's important to train the body and mind. If she's working you like this, just imagine the others" said Master Net

Virgil shook his head "don't remind me" said Virgil

The two began walking back towards the hut in the middle of the forest. As the began approaching the lake Muladhara was sitting on the ground, with Kema in her hands, waiting for them.

"Kema and I have been here for hours waiting for you two" said Muladhara as she glared at Virgil and Master Net.

"She is scary" whispered Master Net

"You don't have to train with her" whispered Virgil

"I can hear you!" shouted Muladhara

"Virgil, take Kema and go wait for me by my tree. I need to speak with Master Net" said Muladhara

Virgil walked up and grabbed Kema from Muladhara "If you're not in the meditative state when I get to you, just prepare to be here all night. Your final test with me begins today and I will not allow you to rest until you pass" said Muladhara.

Virgil let out a sigh and began to walk away "yes ma'am"

When Virgil walked off at a good distance Muladhara turned to Master Net

"We need to talk"

"Okay, is everything alright?" asked Master Net

Muladhara walked over to the nearest tree and sat under it.

"No, my sisters are going to increase the

difficulty of the awakening trails" said Muladhara

"Increase the…the ancestors, they did this!" said Master Net.

Muladhara looked up at Master Net "You knew?" she asked

"Not necessarily, but I do know the ancestor who is really behind Virgil's trails. She is testing him…and me too" said Master Net.

"Who is it?" asked Muladhara

"That I cannot say, she is very particular in who she wants to know of her existence or not."

"Well that's helpful" said Muladhara.

"How long do we have? And how exactly are they going to increase the trails" asked Master Net

"We have until tomorrow, the end of the month. How exactly are they going to increase them? I do not know; I was excused from the meeting when Ajna tested me in front of the others" said Muladhara.

"Hmmm, I see… well no more wasting time. Let's unlock Virgil's first chakra" said Master Net.

Muladhara stood up and nodded her head in agreeance.

Virgil was standing in front of Master Net's hut, with Kema, as the sun's light shone on his forehead and the heat warmed his skin. Kema jumped from Virgil's arms and walked inside of the hut. She turned around and meowed at him, signaling for him to come inside.

"What is it Kema?" asked Virgil

Kema continued to walk forward and Virgil followed along.

Inside of the hut, near the center, was the water hole where Virgil and Master Net sat on the first meeting. The water hole, however, began to glow with a red aura. As if something was shining from deep within the lake. Virgil walked back outside and looked into the water but there was nothing shining or glowing. It was only coming from the water hole in the hut. Virgil walked back inside and saw Kema lying next to the hole. Virgil walked and sat next to her, he looked inside of the hole to see if anything was there. He could he see was that something was definitely down there. The closer he looked, the brighter the red glow became . His pocket than began to glow as well. Virgil turned and reached into his pocket and pulled out the red jasper crystal that Muladhara (Byra) has given him. It was glowing just as bright as the water hole...but what did it all mean.

"It's time for the first test"

Virgil turned around towards the front of the hut and saw Master Net standing at the front.

"Muladhara is outside at her tree entering into deep meditation to prepare for the first test"

Master Net walked over to Virgil and sat in front of him on the other side of the water hole.

"Her energy is soaring...have you not been able to feel it?" asked Master Net.

Virgil looked confused and shrugged his shoulders

"Kema led me into the hut and it was like this. I didn't know I was suppose to feel any type of energy"

Master Net looked intrigued

"Very interesting" said Master Net with a grin.

"Well, the first test is the most important. Muladhara is.."

"The Foundation of all the other chakras and before being acknowledge by the others I must first become one with the root" said Virgil

Master Net looked shocked and amazed "You have been learning, indeed"

"Look, I'm doing this because I still want answers to the things you said to me when we first met" said Virgil "Also, I haven't forgotten about that necklace. Have one waiting for me when I finish all of these tests."

Master Net grinned and nodded his head.

"Okay, so what do I do first?" asked Virgil

With a deep inhale and exhale Master Net looked at Virgil with a serious face.

"Chakra test are not just any ordinary test one goes through in life. You have to be chosen to partake in these tests. These tests are like climbing a tower and at the top you will find a treasure only the divine creator could have created. Inside each test you will gain knowledge of a piece of yourself that you have forgotten that will guide you to this infinite treasure but only if you pass the test. Each test you complete will give you a piece of spiritual wisdom and energy until finally you gain the power to enter into the scared realm...known as the Akashic Records" said Master Net.

"I remember us talking about that place before... when I looked inside of Anahatas leaf" said Virgil.

"Exactly, but there is far more to the Akashic Records than just energy" said Master Net

"What else is there?" asked Virgil

Master Net took another deep inhale through his nose, held it for a few seconds and exhaled through his mouth.

"The records hold any and every type of information known in the universe...Past, Present, and Future. All experiences here on Gaia, what you refer to now as Earth" said Master Net.

Master Net reached into his pocket and pulled out what seemed to be a long two hose pipe, along with a small capsule of powder.

"What's that for?" asked Virgil

Master Net opened the capsule and emptied a small amount of powder into each side of the capsule hose.

"This here, is what is called a tepi. A tepi is used in ancient tribes to administer an ancient plant medicinal herb known as snuff" said Master Net

Virgil looked at the pipe

"So you're going to blow something up my nose?...Nah, I'm good on that" said Virgil

"Before you jump to conclusions let me explain it's purpose...Snuff, is used in ancient practices for many benefits of the brain and overall health. The purpose for it today and in the future is for you to tap into your meditative state without any confusion, negative thoughts or wandering mind. It will help guide you through your test from start to finish" said Master Net.

Virgil looked at the tepi pipe and up at Master Net.

"Will it sting?" asked Virgil

"....Yes, but it will be a quick jolt. As long as you don't inhale through your nose instantly, and choke on the powder. It will surge its way through your nose into the bloodstream, where it will travel to the brain, remove excess mucus and calm the brain, it will allow the pineal gland to do its work and it will place you in a meditative state...Now get into meditation pose" said Master Net.

Virgil crossed his legs and relaxed his body. He closed his eyes and began using the beginning breathwork techniques Master Net had been teaching him. "Control the breath and allow it to flow through the body" said Virgil to himself. As he prepared himself a small gust of wind came flowing through the hut, blowing out all of Master Net's lit candles except for one. Then a familiar voice came to Virgil as he began to relax.

The voice whispered "The journey has begun, we shall meet very soon"

Virgil opened his eyes and looked at Master Net, sitting in front of him.

"Are you ready?" asked Master Net

Virgil nodded his head

Master Net picked up the tepi and slightly leaned over the water hole towards Virgil.

"Allow the power of Gaia to guide you through

the test" whispered Master Net.

Master Net placed the two tepi hose gently in Virgils nostrils. He took a deep breath and when the air in his lungs and stomach reached it's capacity, Master Net blew into the tepi releasing the snuff into Virgil's nose.

Virgil felt a jolt of what seemed to be electricity flowing through his nostrils. It flowed to the top of his head, then to the center and it slowly traveled throughout his whole body. Tears began to fall from his eyes but in just that quick instant, a calm and peaceful wave of energy began to set in throughout his body. He heard the voice of Master Net in the background "Breathe…Just Breathe."

Virgil inhaled the air deeply through his nose, for six seconds, allowing the air to fill his lungs and stomach. He held in the air for three seconds and released it for nine seconds. He continued this technique for several minutes until he heard a small voice in the back of his head say "stop…now relax your breathing" said the voice.

Virgil did as he was commanded and allowed his breathing to return to normal.

"You are no longer in your realm…Welcome to my home" said the voice.

Virgil remained quiet, with his eyes closed and body relaxed.

"Open your eyes Virgil" said the voice.

As commanded Virgil opened his eyes slowly and as his eyes opened, he realized he was no longer inside Master Nets hut … nor was he even on earth anymore.

He was surrounded by darkness, tiny stars, that looked like tiny planets, and in front of him was a tree. A very large tree that very much resembled the cherry blossom tree at Master Aynus Jade Dragon ramen restaurant, except this tree was translucent and bright, with stars instead of leaves on the branches. Each star was designed, colored and made uniquely differently in its own way. Below the tree were seven large roots stretching miles away towards different locations in the void. Virgil stood up and began to approach the tree. On the tree, there were engravings that looked like weird markings. Virgil looked deeper into the tree and saw mixed within the engravings was what looked like a strand…of frozen DNA, following throughout the tree.

"What is this?" asked Virgil

The engravings on the tree began to radiate a dim light. What seemed to be weird markings, were actually drawings. Virgil tried to make out what the images meant but couldn't.

"It say's…Only through you, will our world's come together" said a familiar voice.

Virgil looked up and sitting on one of the top branches of the tree was Muladhara.

"It's written in an old language from ancient times" said Muladhara.

Muladhara jumped from the tree branch and landed behind Virgil. "I've been waiting for you" she said.

Virgil turned and looked at Muladhara "Muladhara…where are we?" asked Virgil as he looked around and turned back to look at the tree.

Muladhara also looked around the dark starry void and back at Virgil.

"We're inside of you of course" said Muladhara

Virgil turned around with a look of confusion

"Inside…of me?" he asked

Muladhara nodded her head "yes indeed" she said.

"This Virgil.. the void.. the stars.. the tree.. everything here is you. Well it's in the beginning stages, but it's all still you" said Muladhara

Virgil turned and looked at the tree "So…this tree…is me?...I thought I'd be taller" said Virgil.

Muladhara began to laugh "You do not listen! Did I not just say it's in the beginning stages?!...If you can pass all seven tests, you'll be amazed of what will happen inside of you" said Muladhara.

Virgil turned, looked at Muladhara and the two made eye contact.

"I'm ready" said Virgil

Muladhara reached both of her hands out towards Virgil, with both of her index fingers touching her thumbs. She continued to stare deep into Virgil's eyes and when the time was right she whispered the word "LAM".

There was a sudden pulse, that shook the void.

What was once a dark void began to turn bright red. The stars turned into crystals and the tree turned into a closed red lotus flower, with a large root stem coming from beneath it.

"Welcome…to the root chakra" said Muladhara.

"Here and before me, you must prove that you are worthy of opening and controlling your root chakra…and to do this.." Muladhara waved her hand in the air and the red lotus flower began to release a small amount of energy from it's core straight into the sky.

"You must sustain the energy coming from the red lotus flower until it has sprouted. The energy coming from this flower is a direct connection of Gaia. In order to continue, your physical body must become one with the earth" said Muladhara.

Virgil turned around and saw a red aura slowly spewing out of the lotus flower.

He felt a shiver travel from the top of his head to the back of his spine. He walked up to the lotus flower and slowly began to reach out towards.

"Wait" said Muladhara.

"Once you touch it…there will be no going

back. There will be a surge of energy charging at you all at once, and you must be able to contain it…"

Virgil took in Muladhara's final words, and without a second thought he placed his hand on the lotus flower and BOOM! A blast of cosmic energy shot straight up from the lotus core. The energy swirled in the voided sky and dashed straight for Virgil. Without a second to think the energy struck Virgil like a red lightning bolt "AAAAHHHHHHH" Virgil screamed out.

Visions of Virgil's past, as a child, began to come to him rapidly. All the pain, hurt, and sadness he felt growing up began to arise again. Virgil fell to his knees as the energy continued to surge through his body. As the energy flowed in the void, the red jasper crystals began to slowly gravitate towards Virgil and began to slowly spin around him. As the crystals spun around a light began to shine in each crystal. As they spun faster and faster around Virgil, an eerie aura slowly began to seep from Virgil's body. Virgil was in too much pain to realize it but the crystals were slowly absorbing the strange eerie aura coming from his body. As everything continued to proceed with Virgil, Muladhara looked up at the lotus flower as it began to bloom.

"It's blooming too slow. At this pace, he'll fail and his body will collapse" said Muladhara.

She then turned her attention back to Virgil and saw that he was still struggling to control the energy.

Virgil, still on his knees, was beginning to feel like his body was going to shatter and collapse. Images of his younger self and the pain he faced growing up were constantly flowing through his head. He was fighting not only his body, but his mind as well. Never had he ever experienced such a surge going through his entire body. As he tried to stand up, the energy pushed him back down, forcing him back on to his knees.

"It's too much...I can't do this" said Virgil to himself

As Virgil tried to stand again, he slowly lifted his head and saw that he was surrounded by a multitude of bright red spinning crystals. The crystals were still absorbing the strange aura from his body. The more the aura came out of his body, the stronger the surge of energy became, and the more Virgil wanted to give up on the test.

As Virgil was prepared to call Muladhara, a voice came to him.

"No, don't do it Virgil!" said the voice

Virgil slowly opened his eyes and saw that standing in front of him, was the little kid version of him.

"No! I won't let you give up!" said little Virgil

Virgil closed his eyes again and fell to his knees.

"Kid…now's not the time" said Virgil

Little Virgil shook his head and walked over to Virgil.

"There's no better time than the present" said little Virgil "Why are you fighting it so much?"

Virgil looked up at his little self

"If..you haven't noticed kid..this hurts…A LOT.." said Virgil

Little Virgil laughed "Of course I know it hurts, I'm you, remember? I just want to know why you're fighting back so hard?" asked Little Virgil

With a deep sigh Virgil slowly opened his eyes and lifted his head.

"How would you like me to handle it?" asked Virgil

"I don't know…I'm just a kid who's watching the older version of himself fight for something he doesn't have to fight so hard for" said little Virgil

You keep fighting the past, and the body, along with the mind, is tiring…sometimes Virgil…you just have to breathe and let it flow" said little Virgil.

Virgil lifted his head and looked at his younger self.

"…Breathe and let it…flow" said Virgil

Realizing what was said, Virgil slowly lowered his body and positioned himself for meditation. As the energy continued to strike, Virgil slowly stopped fighting the energy and relaxed his body.

"Inhale…exhale" said Virgil

"The test isn't about fighting or enduring the pain….it's about letting go and growing from it" whispered Muladhara.

Little Virgil smiled and stood to his feet. He walked through the spinning crystals and up to the red lotus flower. He placed his hands on it and both

Virgil's chanted "I finally accept all of the abundance in my life. My mind, body and spirit are completely nourished. I am now fully grounded."

The red lotus pulsed and sent a wave of energy flowing through the void. The lotus had fully bloomed to perfection, with four large petals sticking out. The crystals stopped spinning and the eerie dark aura had vanished. Virgil continued to sit in meditation with his eye's closed. Muladhara, after witnessing the event, floated over and hovered over the red lotus core.

"Congratulations Virgil...you've passed the root chakras test. I, Muladhara grant you access to the next step."

A bright red light began to shine from Muladhara. Virgil slowly opened his eyes to the red light and as Muladhara slowly vanished she smiled and said "I look forward to seeing you again one day...Virgil"

Virgil closed his eyes as the light became even brighter. The light slowly faded and when Virgil opened his eyes, he was back in the hut with Master Net.

"Congratulation Virgil...you passed" said Master Net.

Virgil looked around the room, it was still dark with one candle lit and the light from the water hole had disappeared.

Virgil turned and looked at Master Net

"How long was I in there?" asked Virgil

Master Net grinned "Time in another dimension is completely different from time here...You've only been meditating for thirty mins" said Master Net.

"thrity mins?! Im...Impossible! I was gone for at least a couple of hours!" said Virgil.

Master Net waved his hand across the air, and all the candles began to light again.

"When you began to meditate and focus your attention onto you root chakra, you were pulled into another realm by Muladhara. A realm that can only be seen deep within you" said Master Net.

Virgil slowly stood to his feet

"How do you feel?" asked Master Net

Virgil looked over into the water hole and saw his reflection staring back at him. He smiled and looked back up at Master Net.

"I feel…that after all this time…I've healed from something that I was running away from…I feel…like a new Virgil"

Master Net stood to his feet and grabbed Virgil and began to hug him.

"Aahaahaa, that's what I wanted to hear!!!" shouted Master Net

"The first step on any journey, is learning to tackle our past trauma. We have to learn to forgive ourselves first, and then others. Then and only then will pain, turn into healing" said Master Net

Master Net pulled back and looked at Virgil

"You are definitely going to be an amazing apprentice young Virgil"

Virgil grinned and put a hand on the back of his head

"Now!! Time for…"

"Tea?" asked Virgil

Master Net laughed "You've learned fast!! Come come!!"

The two walked towards the outside part of the hut. As they walked outside red leaves were falling and swarming the entire forest, covering everything in sight.

"Woah" said Virgil

"This is a sign that you have completed and opened your first chakra" said Master Net.

The two sat down in front of the hut. Master Net had already prepared two cups of tea for Virgil and himself.

"Ginseng tea as usual?" asked Virgil

"Yes indeed!" said Master Net

The two sat and enjoyed their cup of tea, as Muladhara's leaves continued to bless the forest.

"Master Net, there's something I need to ask you" said Virgil

"Yes?"

"When I was deep within meditation, you know in the other realm, inside there was a tree. It looked like the cherry blossom tree, but it was…very different. It had stars instead of leaves, weird markings, that Muladhara said was an ancient language. Oh! And there was frozen, I assume DNA inside of it. What was all that about?" asked Virgil

Master Net took a sip of his tea and looked up at the setting sun.

"Inside of all of us…there is a dormant divine power. It is sleep at the moment, but if you continue on this path…it will awaken" said Master Net

"What exactly kind of power is it?" asked Virgil

"That is something, young apprentice, you will have to find out at the end of the road. The deeper you go within yourself…the more answers you will find" said Master Net.

As the two continued to drink their tea, there was a strange energy that began to creep upon the both of them. Master Net placed his tea down and stood to his feet. "Well so much for a quick breather" said Master Net

"What's happening?" ask Virgil

"Your next teachers are here"

"Wait...Teachers? You mean plural? More than one?" asked Virgil

"Precisely" said Master Net

The red leaves flowing from Muladhara's tree ceased. The sky turned dark and the forest began to speak.

"May the next tests commence..."

Three bright lights began to shine within the forest. Virgil looked around, the orange, yellow and blue sacred trees began to glow. Kema, who had been sleeping on the emerald tree jumped down and ran over towards Master Net and Virgil.

"Why are three trees glowing?!" asked Virgil

"Remain...calm" said Master Net.

Virgil walked to the front of the forest to get a better look of the trees. From each tree walked out three women like entities, shining the same color as their tree, and began to walk towards Virgil.

Master Net walked over towards Virgil and stood next to him.

The three entities stood in front of the both of them in silence.

"Virgil, I would like to introduce you to your next teachers" said Master Net.

"Svad...hishthana? Mani...pura? and Vis...huddha?" asked Virgil

The three entities looked at one another and back at Virgil

"Well done" said Vishuddha

"We are your next teachers who will guide you to opening your sacral, solar plexus and throat chakra" said Manipura

"And with having three teachers at once, the challenges and training will be intensified" said Svadhishthana.

"Are you prepared for the next steps in your journey?" all three sisters asked at once.

Master Net looked at Virgil, Virgil looked down to the ground so no one could see the sweat of nervousness dripping from his face.

"Do you have an answer?" asked Manipura

Virgil looked up with a serious face "I still have a life to live, a job to work but this has been an eye-opening experience...yes, I'm ready"

The three sisters nodded their heads and began walking back to their trees.

"Your training starts tomorrow...you will train with us" said Manipura

"Unlike our sister Muladhara, we will not go see easy on you" said Svadhishthana.

"Muladhara was going easy on me?" said Virgil to himself

The three sisters vanished into the trees and night began to set in. Virgil turned and looked at Master Net.

"So, what are we supposed to do now" asked Virgil

"We call it a night and rest, that is all we can do. Besides you've already done enough for today" said Master Net

As the moonlight shined down on the forest, Virgil turned and saw a white figure sitting underneath the crown chakra tree. The white figure nodded its head at Virgil and vanished into the moonlight.

"I'm going home now..." said Virgil

Virgil began walking out of the forest along with Kema. Master Net stood and watched as both left the forest.

"Master Net….or should I call you by your real name? Master Naki the Neter?" said a woman's voice

Master Net turned around and the white figure, that vanished into the moon, was now standing right behind him.

"I see your apprentice is doing well. Passing the first test is pleasing to the other ancestors. I send him congratulations" said the white figure.

"Good to see you too, old friend" said Master Net

The two approached each other and hugged one another.

"What brings you back to Gaia?" asked Master Net

The white figure looked up at the moon.

"There is a shift coming my dear friend…a major shift….I know you've felt it" said the white figure

"Indeed I have" said Master Net

"I am simply here to…. observe ….and see how this shift will affect the future" said the white figure.

"Interesting…is that all?" asked Master Net.

The white figure turned toward Master Net.

"Your apprentice?...Does he know his role in all of this? Does he know who he is"

"No, he doesn't…I prefer, until he has reached a certain level on journey, to keep all things… a secret. At least until the truth is ready to be revealed" said Master Net

"Understood…I look forward to meeting him one day Naki. Continue to guide him…He has a great teacher" said the white figure.

The white figure began to levitate and glide to the moon.

"The next time we meet Naki…you know what must be done" said the figure as she vanished into the moonlight yet again.

"I know……. I know" said Master Net

Meanwhile, hiding behind a tree was Virgil,

observing everything that took place.

PT. 3

THE INNER TREE

Virgil had begun his training with his next teachers Svadhishthana, Manipura and Vishuddha. As time went by Virgil learned to dive deeper within himself. He learned about his weaknesses that blocked his chakras and changed them into strengths. He continued to work on his body and physique with Master Aynu. He studied meditation, astrology, breathwork, tapped into his inner spirit, sun-gazed and learned his true ancient history with Master Net.

Three weeks of intense training and studying went by and Virgil's growth had begun to show. He was beginning to love who he was becoming.

Virgil, however, was still unhappy because he worked as an assistant teacher at his Elementary School. He loved working with all of his students and sharing the knowledge that he had been learning with them, but deep down inside Virgil knew something needed to change. He could no longer continue to live the same day to day schedule and not see a change in his surroundings. He needed to take control of his life to find his purpose and passion. Something that made him feel that he was actually making a difference but he just didn't know where to start.

On a Friday night, after he had finished his training, Virgil went home, took a cold shower, went outside began to gaze up at the moon. It just so happened to be a full moon out that night, and Virgil remembered what Master Net had continuously told him "The moon has an effect on our emotions and spirit, just as the sun does. Anytime there Is a full moon…always take time to gaze at its beauty and absorb all of its loving energy"

Virgil looked up and his eye's locked with the moon.

"Where do I go from here" asked Virgil

He continued to stare into the sky as the moons light began to shine brightly down unto the earth. Virgil sat down in the grass, slid his sandals off and placed his feet into the ground. He had a journal with him, that his therapist gave him during his first session. He had never used it but something was telling him to open It and start writing. Virgil sat there and began to write everything he had been through from his childhood until now. From feeling alone, hurt, angry, unloved, neglected, and unaccepted from family, past relationships and friends. He began to feel more confident, stronger mentally, physically, emotionally, spiritually and one with himself. He had begun to feel grateful for his life, the people that were still there, growing closer to himself and most of all for being able to learn how to love who he was.

"Lead the children....this Is your gift" whispered a voice.

Virgil looked up at the moon and just like that, he knew what that whisper was for.

"Okay...I'll do It" said Virgil.

He dated and closed his journal, stood to his feet and slid his sandals back on. He walked into his apartment and went to his room. Waiting for him on his bed were three crystals, wrapped in what seem to be copper wire, and on his night stand was a warm cup of tea with a letter next to it. Virgil walked over and picked up the letter. Inside the letter read "You are beginning to find out who you truly are. I know the last 3 weeks training with my sisters have been tough, but I am proud of you Virgil. On your bed you will find a carnelian crystal, a tiger's eye crystal, and lapis lazuli crystal. Each crystal represents one of the chakra's you are currently opening up within you. Allow them to heal you and do their work. Finally, on your night stand you will find a warm cup of tea. This Is a mixture tea of chamomile, blue lotus and calea zacatechichi. Be careful, It Is very bitter! With this tea, allow It to help guide you into the dream world. Look for answers to your questions...you might even see me. I look forward to seeing you again. ASÉ." signed by Muladhara.

Virgil smirked and picked up the cup of tea. The tea was actually not as bitter, mainly because he had begun to get accustomed to the taste. He turned, grabbed the three crystals off of his bed and held them in his palm. He starred at them...and deep within his mind a thought came across his head. "Tap into the crystals?" asked Virgil. He placed the crystal's in different locations in his room. He laid in his bed and continued to sip on his tea. A knock came from his door, and his cousin Cole came into the room. Cole sat down on the edge of Virgils bed and they bumped fist.

"Bro…I just wanted to tell you, you've really changed in these last few months. I don't know what sparked you but it did one heck of a job" said Cole.

"Thanks bro…I….I actually feel better. A lot better. Just had to do some healing from within. I still have a long way to go but I'm grateful for my growth" said Virgil.

"Well, whatever you're doing, send some of that energy my way when you're finished" said Cole "Most definitely" said Virgil.

Cole nodded his head, stood to his feet and left Virgil's room.

Virgil turned off all of the lights in the room and sat on floor. He closed his eyes and took in a deep breath. He began to relax his mind and body while focusing on sacral, solar plexus and throat chakra's.

"Guide me to the realm that lies within me" said Virgil.

A chill began to move from Virgil's lower spine up to his neck. He crossed his legs and had the palm of his hands facing upward. In a split second, the light from the moon shining from the window vanished, and Virgils entire room went dark.

Silence...nothing but silence was left in the room but within that silence, Virgil began to feel the vibration of everything in his body. From his lungs, expanding and releasing the air from his body. To the beat of his heart pumping his blood through his veins. An enormous electrifying chill ran through his spine again. In that moment, his ears began to ring. The ring became louder, and louder the deeper Virgil sinked into his body. Then in an instant, a bright light shined and pushed Virgil into the ground. Virgil's eyes opened and all he could see, where the stars.... bright, beautiful, small stars.

"ee...ee...teee..." said a mans' voice.

Virgil slowly sat up from the ground and in front of him he saw the strange cherry blossom like tree from his last test that had, stars as leaves and frozen DNA inside. This time, however, the DNA was swirling, along with the stars, and seemed to be fused with red, orange, yellow and blue colors. "Woah..." said Virgil. He stood to his feet and began walking to the tree. As he approached the tree, the voice of the man spoke again "ee...ee ...tee...em..he..tep...".

Virgil looked around and saw no one, only the tree. Virgil walked up to the tree and placed his hand on the trunk of the tree.

"Is it you?" asked Virgil

The tree lowered on of it's branches down to Virgil and dropped one of it's stars next to him.

"we...nem.....we...nem" said the man's voice.

Virgil looked down at the star and picked it up. The star slowly changed its shape into the form of a mushroom.

"You want me to hold on to this?" asked Virgil

The tree lowered the branch down to Virgil and pointed at his mouth.

"we...nem.....we....nem" said the man's voice.

Virgil looked at the star and up at the tree.

"You want me to eat this? Asked Virgil

The tree began to shine and the strange DNA within began to swirl faster!

"tee-oo....tee-oo!" shouted the mans voice.

Virgil looked at the mushroom at took in a deep breath. The mushroom began to glow with the colors of the root, sacral, solar and throat chakras. Virgil took a bite out of the mushroom and to his surprise it didn't taste that bad. He then proceeded to eat the whole mushroom until it was gone.

"he...mes...he...mes" said the mans voice.

Virgil turned and looked at the tree "Look I still don't understand you. I don't know that language."

"Sit...down...sit...down" said the man.

Virgil shook his head "Again I don't...wait... I understood you. You said sit down" said Virgil.

"I did...please, sit. We have much to discuss" said the tree.

Virgil nodded and sat down in front of the tree.

"Who are you?" asked Virgil.

"I...am you...a part of you... that has been sleeping for many years" said the tree.

"Asleep? Can you tell me more?" asked Virgil

The ligh, coming from the tree, began to pulse.

"I am a spirit... from an ancient past...that has been sleeping inside of you...for many eons. We have been together...in many different lifetimes. I have seen you grow... from a child...to a man many times" said the tree.

Virgil began to look confused "Wait...are you telling me, I've...I've lived this life before?"

"Absolutely" said the tree "Until you have achieved your purpose, you will continue to live this life. It's is part of your destiny...but...the shift has begun."

"The shift?" asked Virgil

"Yes...the shift" said the tree "The Great Awakening is upon us...and you are one of the chosen. This is why we are here now...having this talk after many years"

"I see...what is your name?" asked Virgil

"That...I can not reveal to you at this moment...

.you must finish unlocking all seven chakras and begin your kundalini activation….only then will I reveal to you who I am, our connection and your purpose" said the tree.

Virgil nodded "I understand"

"But…I am very proud and excited for you…for I have waited for this moment for a very long time…" said the tree

"Thank you" said Virgil "Any wisdom for conquering the other six chakra tests?" asked Virgil.

The tree lowered one of its branches and dropped another mushroom star.

"Svadhishthana, Manipura, and Vishuddha are already aware of your growth. As you can see, your sacral, solar and throat chakras have already opened. For these areas were not your true weakness. The strand of energy inside of me you call DNA has already begun to slowly activate. Now eat more of the food of the spirits" said the tree.

Virgil picked up the mushroom star and ate it. As he chewed the mushroom he looked up at the tree "I have questions…do I still have to take the chakra test? What's going to happen to me when I unlock all the chakras?" asked Virgil

The tree placed one of its branches on top of Virgils head.

"I can no longer give you information...The food of the spirits will guide you now...We shall meet again...Virgil" said the tree.

The tree slowly began to vanish, and then there was nothing but darkness.

Then a strange man's laugh began to slowly fill the void. "Hehehehehe" laugh the man.

"Who's there?" asked Virgil

"Soooooooo....we meet at last Virgil....how I've waited for this moment" said the man. Two loud claps filled the dark void, and before his eyes a torch of fire appeared in front of him with a man wearing a black cloak sitting behind it. In his hands he held three small lotus flowers, each resembling a chakra Virgil was training to unlock.

"Who are you?" asked Virgil

"Ah ah ahhhh" said the strange man "Not before I finish my test"

"Test?" asked Virgil

"Hehehehehhe....the food of the spirits has already begun to take affect and you haven't even noticed" said the strange man.

Virgil looked at him in confusion, Virgil stood to his feet "What are…" Virgil stopped in mid-sentence and looked at his legs. His legs had begun to slightly shake and a warm sensation began to take over. From his feet all the way up to his throat. The warmth took over but it left a very cold spot near his heart.

"Hehehehehe…..now let the games begin" said the strange man

"Games…what games?!" shouted Virgil "What are you doing to my body?" he asked

The cloaked man stood up and walked over towards Virgil. Virgil could no longer feel his body, it had become numb. The cloaked man placed his hand on Virgils shoulder and whispered to him.

"Fall" said the cloaked man.

Without a second thought, Virgils body began to fall backwards and deep into the void it went. Unable to move, unable to shout, unable to do anything, Virgil fell into darkness.

"Welcome to the rabbit hole my friend… because you came here alone, I shall test you to see if you are worthy of receiving the blessing of your sacral, solar and throat chakras ….but wait there's more…Deep in this rabbit hole there is someone waiting for you. Someone very special and if you can find them, you might receive another blessing…hehehehe…This test will drive you mad but only the strong minded can survive…hopefully your brain doesn't fragment and you get stuck here hehehehe…See you on the inside" said the cloaked man as the sound of his laughter echoed throughout the darkness, he watched Virgils body fall deeper into the void.

CHAPTER 5

THE VOID OF DARKNESS

Silence and darkness filled the void as Virgil continued to fall. Paralyzed from his feet to his neck, Virgil had nowhere to go. Fear began to take over Virgil. Not knowing if he would ever wake up from this began to make his heart rush. Stuck in a dark void.... forever was the last thing he'd expect when going within himself. He closed his eyes and embraced darkness. Virgils fall into darkness turned into minutes…minutes turned into hours and hours began to feel like days.

"Hehehehehehe, still falling into darkness, are we?" How deep are you going to journey down this rabbit hole Virgil?"

Virgil opened his eye's and falling in front of him was the strange cloaked man.

"I feel like I've been falling for hours...Who are you and what do you want?" asked Virgil

"Hehehehehe, stuck in a time loop are we? Now if I were to tell you who I am and how to get out of this loop, what fun would that be?" said the cloaked man

"What can you tell me then?" asked Virgil

"Hmmmmmmmmmm...... if you want to know anything about this darkness, this void...you just have to stop falling" said the man

"And how do I do that?" asked Virgil

The cloaked man extended his arm and placed his middle finger in the center of Virgil's forehead.

"This is your world...I'm not going to tell you how to run it...learn how to figure it out" said the man as he disappeared into the void.

Virgil let out a sigh..." I'm getting tired of all of these mind games"

Virgil looked around the void and began to think "hmmmm, if this is my world....then I should be able to…"

Virgil put his hands above his head, closed his eyes and began to imagine a ground. A ground full of soft green grass, moving through his hands, connecting to the soil. Virgil opened his eyes and realized he was no longer falling. He was now holding himself upside down on a small area of green grass.

"Woah…Well I'll be…"

Virgil slowly lowered himself on to the ground, he looked around and realized he was still in the dark void.

"Alright! I stopped falling…now what?" asked Virgil

"Hmmmmmm…why are you Virgil?"

The strange cloaked man was standing behind Virgil back to back.

"Why are you here?" asked Virgil

"Hehehehehe, I'm here because you're here" said the strange man

"Hmm….I don't know why I'm here. I was talking to a tree and then…"

"Ahhhhh, so the tree of life, dwelling within you, sent you here. Hehehehehe, this just became even more interesting" said the strange man.

"Who are.." Virgil turned around and found that the man was gone again, but left a very large mirror in his place.

"Huh?...what is going on?"

Virgil looked in the mirror and saw only his reflection.

Virgil began to stare deep into the mirror, but something was off. The reflection began to act...different.

"Why are you here Virgil?" the reflection asked

"What in…" before Virgil could finish his sentence, his reflection began stepping outside of the mirror.

"WHY ARE YOU HERE VIRGIL!!!" shouted the reflection!

"I…I…I don't know!! Shouted Virgil nervously.

The Virgil reflection smiled "Wrong answer" and kicked Virgil back into darkness.

"Ahhhhhhhhhh!!!" screamed Virgil as he began to fall again.

The reflection watched as Virgil began to fall deeper in the void of darkness.

"Until you understand why you're here" the reflection shifted it's form into that of the strange cloaked man "I'll never let you leave this place, hehehehehehe" laughed the man.

Virgil began to fall deeper and deeper into the void. The further he went the stranger it became. Voices began talking to him, calling out his name "Virgil! Virgil! Virgil!"

"Leave me alone...Leave me alone....LEAVE ME ALOOONNNEEE!!!!" shouted Virgil

Trapped in the void, there was no escape...there was only darkness...and fear began to take over.

"Why am I here?....someone...please help me"

From deep within the void, Virgil heard the laughter of a child.

"Hello?...who's there?...Hello?" called Virgil

"How did we end up in this place" asked the child

Virgil slowly turned his head and saw that it was the younger version of himself falling next to him.

"Little Virgil, what are you doing here?"

"I mean, we are the exact same person you know. Wherever you go I am with you. I just don't go POOF after we finish talking......or do I?" said little Virgil

"That's besides the point, how did we get here Virgil?" asked Little Virgil

"I...I don't...wait...that tree...it was talking to me...it gave me those strange looking mushrooms ... it told me to eat them" said Virgil

"Mhmmmmm, okay so we're taking strange food from trees now...whew how we've forgotten Master Net's teachings already"

"Hush little Virgil...this isn't the time...let's first stop falling"

"Okay!" shouted little Virgil

Little Virgil closed his eyes and began to wave his hands around.

"Stop" said Little Virgil

Both Virgil's, at that moment, stopped falling.

"Home" said Little Virgil

Out of the void, a medium size green house appeared in front of the Virgil's.

"We're home!" shouted little Virgil

Little Virgil rushed into the house,

"Mmhmmmmmm, so this is where you grew up? I wonder what secrets are inside" said the strange cloaked man as he appeared next to Virgil.

Virgil turned and looked at the man "I don't know who you are...but you're really starting to irritate me"

"That's perfect, I wouldn't be doing my duty if I didn't" said the cloaked man.

They both began walking towards the house.

"Why is it green?" asked Virgil to himself. "My house was never green".

The two walked into the house where little Virgil was waiting for them in the living room area.

"You!! Who are you!?!" shouted Little Virgil as he pointed at the strange man.

The man walked over to Little Virgil and stood over him.

"You really want to know who I am?" asked the man

A cold shiver went down little Virgils spine.

"Nope, never mind. I'm good" said Little Virgil as he slowly walked over to the original Virgil

Virgil walked around the living room and began observing the house. The living room furniture was still the same, it actually looked brand new. There were pictures on the walls of Virgils family and life growing up. Memories from his past began to set in.

"This house...many memories I have in here. Good, bad, ugly....painful" said Virgil

"Ahhhh, painful you say?" asked the strange man.

"Yea...painful. Being in here sometimes...just makes me feel"

"Uncomfortable?" said the strange man

Virgil turn and looked at him "Yes... uncomfortable ...did you know that I was coming here?" asked Virgil

"Hehehehehehe, pointless questions. Let us...explore this uncomfortable past of yours, shall we?"

The strange man ventured off into the house.

"He really gives me the creeps" whispered Little Virgil

"Join the club" said Virgil as he followed behind the strange man

"You're...you're actually going with him?" asked Little Virgil

"He knows something...and I need to find us a way out of here" said Virgil

"Out of all times for me to poof up, we end up in a dark void, following a strange creep in a house...those two just don't mix!!" said little Virgil as he followed along

The three of them wandered around the house, going from room to room.

"Mhmmmm, there is definitely much trauma and energy still in these rooms...much pain, much hurt, much...anger" said the strange man

Virgil walked up to a family portrait hanging in

the hallway.

"Growing up, I was very disconnected from my family. I felt alone and different from them. My twin little sister's, we were ten years apart. My mother was nice but just felt like she didn't get me. My father...we just never connected...I stayed to myself a lot. I stayed in my head. Never knew how to express myself, my emotions, my thoughts to them" said Virgil

The strange man walked up to Virgil "Well then...lets fix that now"

He clapped his hands 3 times, and everyone was back in the living room area.

However, this time, they weren't alone. Virgil's father, mother, and sisters were sitting on the living room couch waiting for him.

"...why are they here?" asked Virgil

"Who knows, the void sometimes has a mind of its own" said the strange man

Virgil walked over to his family and sat in front of them.

"Why are you here?" asked Virgil

"The same reason why you're here" said Virgil's family

Virgil turned and looked at little Virgil. He shrugged his shoulders and walked over next to him.

"You've truly grown into an amazing man" said Virgils father

"and an amazing son" said Virgils mother

"and an amazing brother" said Virgils sisters

Virgil just looked at them and didn't know how to respond.

"Whatever you're holding onto son, let it out. It's okay, you're ready" said Virgils father

Virgil looked at them and his eyes started to get watery

"Why...why am I so angry with you all...why am I so hurt...I'm tired of carrying all of this...I just want to be done" said Virgil

Virgils mom reached out and grabbed his hands

"Virgil...you have held on to so much pain and hurt from when you were younger to now. From not having a connection to your father like you wanted. To not ever bonding with your sisters because you felt like they were treated better. To me not allowing you to live your life the way you wanted to......It's time to let it all go son" said Virgils mother

"That's the thing mom...how? How do I let go of all the hurt...the pain. I've carried so much more inside of me, for so long"

"That's the thing Virgil...you don't have to anymore. This is your life, your story, your reality. If you want to hold on, that's up to you son. If you want to let go, you just have to let go...That's why you're here...that's why we're all here. Let go of all the pain from the past...so you can finally be free" said Virgils mother

"You're a man now son...learn from your past...don't dwell in it. Doing that will only hold you back...and if you ever need guidance, I know I messed up when you were younger, but as your father...I'm here for you son"

"And even though we annoy you, and aggravate you, we really appreciate our big brother. We need him more than we think. We love you" said Virgils sisters

Virgil sat up and looked at his family and smiled.

"Thank you...thank you my family" said Virgil

The family disappeared along with the house. Nothing was left but Virgil, little Virgil and the strange man.

"Mhmmmm, the void of darkness...always taking people to their unresolved issues" said the strange man.

Little Virgil looked up at Virgil and put his hand on his shoulder.

"How do you feel?" asked Little Virgil

Virgil stood to his feet and cleared his face.

"I haven't felt this good in a long time" said Virgil

Little Virgil stood up next to him and nodded his head.

"Hmmmm, so where will the void take you now?" asked the strange man.

Then from within the darkness, a voice called

out to Virgil.

"Virgil…" whispered a woman's voice

Virgil began to look around the void and saw nothing.

"Virgil…" whispered the woman's voice again.

"Do you all not here that?" asked Virgil

"Here what?" asked Little Virgil

Virgil turned around and standing a few feet away from him was a green door.

"How…never mind" said Virgil

A path formed and stretched all the way to the door.

"I believe this door, is only for one" said the strange man

Virgil looked down at Little Virgil

"Stay here…he won't hurt you" said Virgil as he began to follow the path

Little Virgil looked at the strange man and back Virgil

"Are you sure" asked Little Virgil

"I'm sure" said Virgil "I know who he is now"

The strange man nodded his head and watched Virgil as he approached the door.

When he arrived at the door, there was a message carved into it waiting for him.

It read "Be warned…Only enter if you are truly ready to Let Go of the Past"

Virgil turned around and nodded his head at the strange man and little Virgil.

He turned to the door, grabbed the doorknob and began to walk through.

On the other side of the door Virgil entered into a room…a very familiar room.

"How…why am I here?" asked Virgil.

The door quickly shut itself and disappeared.

"Wait! Wait! Not here! Not Here! I'm not ready!" shouted Virgil

"Hello…. Virgil" said a woman's voice.

Virgil froze up and slowly began to turn around.

However, what he said was not what he

expected. Floating in front of him was a small green orb with a strange symbol in the middle of it.

"I know that symbol" said Virgil

"I would hope you do know of me Virgil…we finally meet at last. Well…in my original form that is. I see you've been exploring the void of darkness. You've done well" said the orb.

"….Anahata…why? how? I'm confused" said Virgil

"Calm yourself Virgil…this is all part of the process" said Anahata.

"I've been waiting for this moment for a very, very long time.

"Why am I here Anahata? Specifically…WHY AM I IN THIS ROOM?!" asked Virgil frantically

Anahata giggled and proceeded towards Virgil.

"First off, I am the heart chakra Anahata, you should know love is my power. Also did you not read the sign that was left for you? It warned you not to enter unless you were truly ready"

"It wasn't like I had any choice" whispered Virgil

"We all have a choice…and this was yours. No going back now" said Anahata.

"Now, allow us to venture deeper into your life…much to see…much to discuss…much to let go" said Anahata.

"But first, allow me to be in a more familiar form to you, that you will be more comfortable with"

Anahata floated towards the ground and began to emit a bright light. As the light shined brighter Virgil slowly put his hand up and turned his head. When the light slowly faded Virgil turned as was surprised to see none other than Kema sitting in front of him.

"Wait…you've been"

"Precisely" said Anahata

"Wait how are you talking to me right now" asked Virgil

"Telepathic energy waves, we all have them, but that's a discussion for another day" said Anahata

Virgil walked up to Anahata "So you've been Anahata and Kema this whole-time…but why?"

"How?? I'm still working and training with the others. Why are you here?" asked Virgil

"You've already passed their test Virgil....that is why you're here with me now" said Anahata

Virgil now looking confused "I...I haven't done anything"

"Oh but you have" said Anahata "You have actually surpassed all of our expectations. The tests that you would have taken with my other sisters would have led you right here...into the void of darkness. All roads on this journey lead to the darkness that is within us. That is where the most growth can take place. But with that powerful spirit sleeping inside of you, it was only a matter of time".

"Sleeping spirit?" asked Virgil

"Indeed, but you will learn more about that soon...until then, we have much to explore inside of you Virgil. Your other chakras have already begun to activate, but there is a blockage inside of you...a very strong blockage" said Anahata as she snapped her fingers twice.

"I Anahata, the heart chakra, will be your guide within the final test of the void of darkness. No more running from hurt…it is time to rise" said Anahata

"If there's one thing I know…I know exactly who you are Virgil. Revealing myself to you in the beginning would not have been the wisest decision, but I will say this… I've been with you for many years and I have been waiting for this moment. Protecting you from unseen forces and watching you grow. I've seen you grow from a small boy to now this amazing man. You've done in such a short amount of time Virgil" said Anahata

Virgil had nothing to say…he was speechless. From afar there was a loud door slam and yelling going on in another room.

"Ahhhhh, I even know why you're nervous of being in this exact room at this moment" said Anahata

Virgil turned and looked at the closed bedroom door. There was a lot of yelling and arguing going on in the next room.

"Out of all days…out of all events…why this one?" asked Virgil

Anahata looked up at him "Because it's time to

let it go"

Virgil walked to the door and opened it. The door lead into the living room and in there was Virgil and a woman arguing"

"If I am correct this is your recent last girlfriend, correct" asked Anahata

"Indeed" said Virgil

The two watched the argument as it began to get heated.

"Why are you like this?! All I ask is that you understand where I'm coming from?!" said younger Virgil

"Understand?! Understand?! You know what I'm trying to understand why are you such a sensitive MAN!!! GROW UP, GROW SOME TOUGH SKIN AND GET OUT OF YOUR FEELINGS!!! said the woman.

"Why are you acting like this yo?! Like seriously! All I'm asking is for you to understand my point and hear me out! Learn how to adapt and change in this relationship nothing is always going to stay the same! We are constantly changing and growing, we have learn new ways to approaching each other! We have to learn to grow with each other!" said younger Virgil

"You know what Virgil, you're right...but I'm not changing for no man. I'm going to be me at the end of the day, either you love me for that, or get to steppin. I've done my part, I've tried to love you the best way that I can and it just ain't working out. You can leave go find you someone else, cool no hard feelings, but this, I'm not with it". said the woman

"Let's pause this moment right here" said Anahata "Explain to me, what's going on here" she asked.

Virgil let out a sigh "We...We were having an argument over some things that we had been dealing with. This particular argument got out of hand. It's like all that love and energy we had for each other disappeared...it was more like looking at my enemy and not my friend" said Virgil.

"Hmmmm interesting..." said Anahata "Let's try this out..."

Anahata glared at the woman, and a light began forming around her, changing her into another Virgil.

"Instead of us watching an argument with you and your ex, let's see how things look when you are arguing with yourself" said Anahata.

"What is this going to prove?" asked Virgil

"Shhhhhhhh! Just watch"

""Why are you like this?! All I ask is that you understand where I'm coming from?!" said one Virgil

"Understand?! Understand?! You know what I'm trying to understand why are you such a sensitive MAN!!! GROW UP, GROW SOME TOUGH SKIN AND GET OUT OF YOUR FEELINGS!!! said the other Virgil.

"Why are you acting like this yo?! Like seriously! All I'm asking is for you to understand my point and hear me out! Learn how to adapt and change in this relationship nothing is always going to stay the same! We are constantly changing and growing, we have learn new ways to approaching each other! We have to learn to grow with each other yo!" said Virgil

"You know what Virgil, you're right...but I'm not changing for no man. I'm going to be me at the end of the day, either you love me for that, or get to steppin. I've done my part, I've tried to love you the best way that I can and it just ain't working out. You can leave go find you someone else, cool no hard feelings, but this, I'm not with it". said the other Virgil.

"Pause…. shift back" said Anahata

The Virgil copy switched back into the woman.

"Woah…that hits different" said Virgil

"Indeed…see Virgil, all this time you've been doing nothing but arguing with yourself. You just…couldn't see it." said Anahata

"What are you talking about?" he asked.

Anahata walked over to the arguing couple.

"Everyone that has ever came into your life, whether it be this woman, or another from your past, or even a friend…have all been just different versions of you" said Anahata.

"I'm so confused…" said Virgil

Anahata giggled "Of course you are but let me explain. When someone comes into your life, what is it that attracts them to you?"

"Uhhhh, I don't know, their personality, their mind, and their looks I guess" said Virgil

Anahata shook her head "typical, human answer...I want you to look deeper Virgil"

Virgil looked at his ex and himself. He walked up to them and continued to look at them.

"I wonder...." Virgil looked at his hands and placed one on his ex and another on himself.

Virgil looked at Anahata and nodded his head.

"Energy...we came together because my energy attracted her, and her energy attracted me."

"Precisely" said Anahata "Energy, frequencies and vibrations are the focus of all things. You released a certain frequency, her energy felt it, and brought her to your energy. The vibrations inside of both of you communicated and connected.... nothing in this world, in this reality is by coincidence" said Anahata

"So what, what does any of that have to do with this situation?" asked Virgil

"Mhmmmmmm, you attract these people into your life for one reason and one reason only, to learn and discover something about yourself that will help you on your path towards growth. Many and I mean many, humans fail to realize this. They sometimes take these lessons and encounters deeper than what they should be, all in the name of love" said Anahata.

"But...isn't love the reason why we stay with that person?" ask Virgil. He turned a looked at his ex "I can genuinely say...I deeply loved this woman. I wanted to be the best man I could for her. I had flaws, but I was willing to grow and work on those...for me...for us" said Virgil.

"And that alone was your lesson Virgil. Actually there were many lessons in this relationship you failed to realize" said Anahata.

"Like what? What other than not being too sensitive or be a better man did I miss?"

Anahata locked eyes with Virgil and transformed herself into his ex-girlfriend.

"Listen and listen well to the wisdom of Anahata. As a man, you cannot love someone until you yourself have found and established your path in life. A man's first duty is to find himself, follow his purpose and grow into being a man…no a King. Then and only then will he be able to give himself to a woman. As a spirit, you cannot love another spirit until you have given your spirit that true meaningful unconditional love. You must learn to love yourself, every part, every flaw, all the good, all the bad, the masculine and the feminine. Self-Love is truly the first love and after that, everything else will come…now…it's time to let go and grow Virgil" said Anahata and she changed back into her original form.

As Virgil listened to Anahata's words he began to feel his eyes watering up. For the first time ever…he felt free from all the hurt he had been carrying. Free from all the past pain of loving someone and giving his all. Free from not feeling that he was ever good enough. Free from overthinking, overanalyzing, being overly emotional …He felt free.

Virgil returned back in the void where the strange man and little Virgil were waiting for him. Anahata turned and saw the strange man standing with little Virgil.

"I believe they are waiting for you" said Anahata

Virgil turned, smiled and began walking towards them with Kema.

"So you finally made it out. I was starting to think I would have to send the kid in there to get you" said the strange man

"Virgil never leaves me around the guy again" said Little Virgil

Virgil smiled and walked up to the two

"Little man you were safe, even if he is a creep …he would have never hurt you. Am I right…. Virgil?"

Little Virgils eye's got wide "Wait..what?!"

"Hehehehehehe, so you figured it out" said the strange man

The strange man removed the cloak from over his head. It was none other than Virgil, just a little older.

"Well isn't this interesting" said Anahata "The past is witnessing his light and dark sides meeting for the first time"

"I'm not such a creepy old man, but I have to adhere to the void of darkness and it's rules" said shadow Virgil "You did well Virgil...you're almost there...and I can't wait to see your face when you find out the truth"

"So...this is it?" asked Virgil

"We will definitely meet again, my friend. After all, I am you. You don't want to stay in the void for too long. You begin to find things out you wish you never did, and we don't need your brain fragmenting now do we" said cloaked Virgil "By the way, these are yours"

Shadow Virgil handed regular Virgil three lotus flowers resembling his sacral, solar, and throat chakra.

"Because you were able to pass this test, you are blessed with these chakra lotus flowers that show you have unlocked these chakras" said cloaked Virgil

Virgil took the lotus flowers and held them in his hands. The lotus flowers began emit a small light, and pulse as if a heart was beating.

"I will now be returning you back to the surface world" said Anahata "Ready?"

"Yea...I'm ready" said Virgil

"Me too!" said Little Virgil

Virgil walked over and hugged shadow Virgil.

"Thank you" said Virgil

Anahata began to release her energy within the void, until it was covered in her light.

The light got brighter and brighter, to finally it blinded everyone in the void.

When the light finally calmed Virgil opened his eyes, and he was now back in his room, with the sun shining right through his window.

"That was a very long night" said Virgil

Virgil stood up and laid in his bed to allow his body to rest and recover.

A few days went by and Virgil was in his car taking a drive. He knew he had some unresolved business. Virgil pulled up to a house and turned the car off. He got out and walked up to the door. He took in a deep sigh and ranged the doorbell. When the door opened, Virgil smiled at who was on the other side.

"....Virgil?"

"Hey mama" said Virgil

She opened the door and wrapped her arms around him.

"You finally came home"

"Yea, I finally came home" said Virgil

PT. 2

THE COMING SHIFT

Deep in the galaxy there is sacred pyramid, on the planet Titan, where three beings have come together to meet on the soon coming events. "We meet again Crown Chakra Sahasrara" said one of the beings.

Sahasrara turned and greeted the spiritual being "Greetings...last time we met was in the Akashic Records. May I ask why you decided to meet here on Pluto?" asked Sahasrara.

"It is because I requested it" said a mans voice. Sahasrara and the other beings turned, and standing in front of them was a giant being in a cloaked outfit hiding his face.

"It has been a very long since we have seen each other" said the man

"Ahhhh, it has been a long time indeed your majesty" said Sahasrara

The giant man turned and looked at the other being.

"In my presence you do not have to continue hiding yourself Queen, only the three of us are here" said the man

The being nodded and with a quick flash a light the being revealed herself to the two.

"Hmm, all this time I never knew it was you Ma'at...Good to see you again sister" said Sahasrara

"My identity being kept secret is very important ...there are beings in this universe that will do anything to stop this shift" said Ma'at

"As long as I am here...No being or entity will approach you. Please let us sit" said the man. All three sat around a large table, "Sahasrara, how are the final preparations for the boy coming along?" asked the man

Sahasrara waved her hand in the air, and an image of a tree, similar to Virgils, appeared.

"Virgils tree has begun to slowly unlock and activate his DNA. He has passed the Root and Heart chakra test, and was able to surpass the Sacral, Solar and Throat test by entering into the Void of Darkness ahead of schedule" said Sahasrara

"He already entered into the Void!" shouted Ma'at

"Indeed...apparently he had some assistance from his inner spirit" said Sahasrara

The man began to grin "Mmmmmmm, so he's finally waking up. Ahh, how I am ready to see him awaken" said the man

"Ajna is ready to take him to the next step and unlock his third eye. However she has been very rebellious towards him since he began this journey" said Sahasrara

Ma'at looked at Sahasrara "I will talk to her, we have a very close relationship from when I was on Gaia"

"Understood" said Sahasrara

The tall man waved his hand over the table and images of all the planets in the solar system popped up.

"The great shift is upon us, many have been preparing for this and it is up to you two to make sure the boy is ready. As you can see the energy from the planets is moving through the galaxy" said the cloaked man

"Understood" said Sahasrara and Ma'at

"The awakening is coming, do what must be done…or Gaia will suffer major consequences" said the cloaked man.

The doors to the pyramid opened and another tall man walked into the pyramid room.

"Master…it's time for you to return back to Nibiru my lord" said the tall man

"Ahh, duty calls my sisters. Sahasrara, Ma'at we shall meet again my friends"

The tall cloaked man stood up and walked out of the pyramid.

Sahasrara and Ma'at looke at each other nodded.

I will return back to the Akashic Records, I will

let you handle my sister Ajna. Be quick, we shall begin Virgils next phase soon" said Sahasrara

"Understood, I will be there to over see that this test goes smoothly" said Ma'at

The two stood up and exited the pyramid. As they walked out of the pyramid they observed a small ship flying off into the distance deep into the galaxy.

"Do you remember when this planet was home to them?" asked Sahasrara

"I do...and it will be home to many again, one day soon" said Ma'at "This entire galaxy is about to change"

CHAPTER 6

AJNA AND THE SERPENTS

Several weeks passed since Virgil entered into the void of darkness. After returning back he told Master Net what had happened, and Master Net was furious. For Virgil to enter the void on his own and not fully understanding what the void was at the time, was a foolish move. Virgil could have been trapped there forever and stuck in infinite darkness. However, because of the guidance of Anahata, Virgil was able to make it back without causing any damage to his psyche. Now that he had begun tapping into himself and learning to go within, Master Net saw this as a perfect time to begin Virgil's training on his last two chakras. He summoned a meeting with Sahasrara to begin working out plans for Virgil's final test. Meanwhile Virgil was to meet with Svadhishthana, Manipura, Vishuddha, and of course Kema, who had been Anahata the Entire time, to update them on his growth and training. Knowing that he had already been through the void, this sisters saw that it was only right to test all of his chakras before continuing on. Svadhishthana ordered Virgil to train on his creativity by following one of his long-lost passions of being an artist and at anytime he needed to restore his chakra, he could sit by the element water. Manipura requested that Virgil continue to build his confidence and learn to not let his ego interfere or take control over him in future events. The element of fire would guide him, if he ever needed guidance for his solar chakra. Finally, Vishuddha asked Virgil to learn to express himself and communicate with his true voice and stop allowing others to control his voice. If he ever needed her, he could find her in the sky with the element air. Once the three sisters left their requests with Virgil they walked to their trees, turned, nodded at Virgil and disappeared into their trees. Kema, on the other hand, stayed by Virgil's side, for her work was not quite done. The two walked off to the front of the forest and met with Master Aynu, who had been waiting for Virgil to start his physical training.

"You're late Virgil!" shouted Virgil

"Yes, I know Master Aynu. I was meeting with the chakra sister's for the last time. Apologies" said Virgil

"Hmm, excuses. Go, begin you kundalini yoga poses and we will begin your strength training afterwards, or should I make you run for the whole day?" asked Master Aynu

Virgil let out a sigh "No Master" Virgil walked over to the giant cherry blossom tree and began doing his poses. Meanwhile, Kema ran over and climbed to the top of the tree and decided to take a nap. Master Aynu nodded his head and continued to drink his warm ginseng tea.

Meanwhile, deep in the sacred forest, Ma'at had summoned a meeting with Ajna to discuss the coming events.

"No...I refuse to train him or even test him Ma'at" said Ajna

"Now Ajna, you and I both know you are one of the most important sister's when it comes to this test. The fate of Gaia is at stake here my friend" said Ma'at

"Gaia has been corrupted for too long. I trust none of those humans. They have been destroying her for years. Maybe it's time she resets them all once again. Start from scratch!" said Ajna

Ma'at sighed and walked over to Ajna "My friend, you know just as well as I do, that even if Gaia resets again, there will still and always be corruption. It's part of the balance" said Ma'at

Ajna turned and looked deep within Ma'ats eyes "tell me, why should I allow this boy to achieve activation? Why does he matter so much?" asked Ajna

Ma'at smiled "Because he will be one of many amazing humans to make this planet better for all beings in this universe...and he can only do that with your help Ajna. Besides...the king of Nibiru has requested you do this" said Ma'at

Ajna eyes widen "The King?! He's a part of this as well?!"

"Indeed...this boy means a lot to him and many of the others on that planet" said Ma'at

Ajna turned and punched the ground sending a surge of energy through the forest.

"Anger is not a common trait of one of the chakra sister's Ajna, and you know this"

Ajna stood up from the ground and began to walk away.

"Ajna!" shouted Ma'at

Ajna stopped and slowly turned her head, looking out of the corner of her eyes at Ma'at

"If you really and truly want to help Gaia, pass all of your knowledge and teachings to the boy. Look within him, and show him the things on this planet that anger you so, so he can make the changes my friend. You have so much to give Ajna…don't allow this world to crumble when you can make real difference" said Ma'at

Ajna turned and began to walk away into the forest. Ma'at watched until Ajna was no longer in her sight. She looked up into the sky and said a prayer.

"My dear and beloved family continue to be patient. Everything is coming together. You, I and all of us shall be free and at peace very soon"

Ma'at vanished into the forest after saying her prayer and a surge of wind soared through the forest. The wind was so powerful that it reached the front of the forest knocking Virgil out of his yoga poses, Kema from the top of the tree onto Virgils back and spilling all of Master Aynus tea.

"What was that all about?" asked Virgil

Master Aynu stood and turned towards the forest

"Something is carrying a lot of anger in there" said Aynu

Virgil stood to his feet and walked over next to Master Aynu.

"Should we go check it out?" he asked

Aynu shook his head "With a wind surge like that roaring through the forest, we are better off waiting for Master Net to return. Something is very…off.

Virgil nodded his head "Understood"

Aynu looked up at Virgil "That doesn't mean you're off the hook from your training! Back to work"

Virgil sighed "Yes master" and went back over to the cherry blossom tree to continue to train.

Master Aynu looked at Kema and called her over. Kema walked over to Aynu and hopped on his shoulder.

"Kema...I want you to go and investigate that surge of wind. It felt like it came from one of the seven sisters of the forest"

Kema meowed and hopped off of Aynus shoulder and began walking into the forest.

Aynu walked over and began cleaning up his spilled tea. He turned and looked at Virgil "You're being lazy with it, START OVER!!" he shouted

Virgil groaned "Yes master"

Aynu shook his head and continued to clean.

Deep within the forest Keam was approaching the center where the seven chakra trees were located. All the trees seemed to be intact except for two. Ajnas and Muladharas trees were activated. She walked over and saw both sisters standing face to face with each other. As Kema began to approach them, Ajna saw and shouted "This doesn't concern you sister!! Stay back!"

"Don't you dare yell at Anahata like that Ajna! What is wrong with you sister!?" asked Muladhara

"You! All of you! How dare you continue to allow another human grow closer to activation knowing none of them are no longer good! He will betray you all! Just like others have!! shouted Ajna

"Ajna…sister, you can't do this as one of the chakra sisters. You have to stop or…"

"Or what?!" shouted Ajna "You're going to stop me? Hahahah" laughed Ajna

"I Muladhara one of the seven chakra sisters will do what I must in order to keep the balance" said Muladhara

"You're a fool too" said Ajna as she charged for Muladhara to attack her.

"I'm done with all of you! None of you can see what I see!!! Shouted Ajna

"Wrong" said Muladhara "You might be the third eye chakra, but I can see very clearly"

Ajna went in to throw a surge of energy at Muladhara and with no hesitation a bright green light of energy shot at Ajna sending her several feet back away from Muladhara.

Ajna stood to her feet and was shocked to see Anahata standing next to Muladhara.

Muladhara turned and her eyes widened. "Anahata…you've…you've never taken this form before" said Muladhara

Anahata had changed into her original chakra form that all sisters are given at the beginning. Chakra sisters have the ability, over time, to either look more humanoid or change into animals while blending in with other living beings on Gaia. Their original form is more divine and of the cosmos, while still resembling the shape of a human without the features. Sisters take this form when true order must be restored.

Anahata had not taken this form in thousands of years but only because of her love for the cats on Gaia.

"You have gone too far Ajna" said Anahata "How dare you make me take this form on you out of everyone"

Angry now at both of her sisters, Ajna stood to her feet.

"It matters not that you have taken your divine form. Neither of you can or will stop me" said Ajna

Ajna charged for both of them again and full speed with all her power.

Anahata looked at Muladhara "You know what to do sister"

Muladhara nodded her head and charged at Ajna while summoning her energy from the earth. The two sisters collided and began to fight one another. The forest began to become upset and dark clouds in the sky began to form. Anahata looked up at the sky "I do apologize Gaia. This will not take long"

She held both of her hands up facing towards Ajna and Muladhara.

"Divine Cosmos, lend me your energy so that I may stop my confused sister" said Anahata.

Meanwhile, in the front of the forest Virgil had finished doing his yoga poses and stood to his feet. He looked up in the sky and saw that a dark cloud was hovering only over the forest.

"Uhhh Master Aynu...do you see that?" asked Virgil

"I see that you....stopped...training...what is going on?" asked Aynu

Without a second thought Virgil took off into the forest

"Virgil no! Wait!" shouted Aynu but it was too late

Virgil ran as fast as he could to the heart of the forest. When he arrived he couldn't believe what he was seeing.

"Muladhara? Is that Anahata? And who is that?! What's...What's going on?" he asked himself.

He saw that both Ajna and Muladhara had been fighting each other while Anahata stood there holding her hands up at both of them.

Ajna and Muladhara continued to fight but Muladhara was beginning to run out of energy.

"I've never had to use this much energy before" said Muladhara to herself

"At this rate, I'm not going to make it for too long"

Ajna stopped, looked at Muladhara and began to grin "What's wrong sister? I thought you could keep up!!" she shouted while charging full force with all of her energy.

"Muladhara!!!" shouted Virgil

Muladhara and Anahata turned, and were both shocked to see Virgil.

"Virgil? No!! Get out of.." before she could finish her sentence Muladhara was knocked straight into the ground by Ajna.

"Hmm, too weak and too caring sister" said Ajna.

"Get away from her!!" shouted Virgil rushing towards Ajna

"I'll definitely be happy to end you as well boy! Besides this is all your fault anyway!!" shouted Ajna.

Virgil tried to hit Ajna but she was too fast and she instantly knocked him to the ground.

"Hmph, pitiful and they wanted me to train you? You were unworthy from the moment I saw you" said Ajna

Virgil laid there unconscious next to Muladhara. Anahata continued to stay there holding her hands at Ajna.

"Please cosmos, lend me your strength" said Anahata

Ajna looked at Virgil and held her hand at him.

"This world needs to reset, and without you…it will" said Ajna

As she began to send energy to the palm of her hand, she looked up at Anahata.

"Keep trying all you want sister. You've already lost" said Ajna

She looked back down at Virgil and saw that a greenish aura had started to form over him. The aura began to glow, and Virgil began to slowly stand to his feet.

"No…I won't allow this!" shouted Ajna sending a wave of energy towards Virgil but the energy ceased before it could reach him.

Ajna was shocked and could not understand what had just happened. She sent another energy wave and another and another but none of them were working.

"You just don't understand…do you Ajna of the third eye chakra?" asked Virgil

Virgil opened his eyes and his eyes were all white and glowing.

"You...you aren't the boy...you're him" said Ajna

"You know who I am Ajna...and you have now angered me" Virgil turned, looked at Anahata and sent an enormous amount of energy her way "Anahata of the heart chakra...do it"

"Yes" said Anahata

Ajna turned and looked at Anahata but it was too late.

"Divine Pyramid, Cosmic Seal!" shouted Anahata

Anahata sent a tremendous amount of energy towards Ajna, sealing her inside what looked like a triangle.

"Sahasrara will decide what to do with you now" said Anahata

She walked over towards Virgil and kneeled to him.

"That is unnecessary Anahata of the heart chakra. You may stand before me" said the spirit inside of Virgil

Anahata stood to her feet "Yes your majesty, it is good to see you again"

"Good to see you as well" said the spirit "But this is only short lived, this boys body was not ready for this much energy and he will now have to rest for a few days to recover. Speak not of what happened here to anyone and continue to take care of this boy" said the spirit

"Understood" said Anahata

"Good, now please attend to Muladhara of the root chakra and this boy's body. I shall return back to sleep...Until next time Anahata" said Virgil as his began to fall to ground. His eyes stopped glowing and the greenish aura disappeared from his body. As soon. As soon as everything was over Master Net and Sahasrara appeared from the crown chakra tree.

"Wha...What has happened?!" shouted Master Net

He ran over to Virgil to check on him, along with Sahasrara

"Virgil...Virgil...wake up my boy...Virgil!" said Master Net

"He needs much rest Master Net but he will be

fine" said Anahata

"What has happened here sister....and why have you entered into your divine form? You haven't done that in years" asked Sahasrara

Anahata pointed at Ajna now sealed inside the cosmic energy.

"Ajna went on a rampage of anger, Muladhara and I both tried to stop her, along with Virgil. I was able to seal her away until you were able to arrive here" said Anahata

Sahasrara turned and walked over to Ajna

"Ajna...how could you my sister?" said Sahasrara

With a sigh she turned towards Anahata "She will have to stand among the other sisters and be judged for her actions. It is prohibited for seven chakra sisters to fight amongst each other"

Anahata nodded her head in agreeance.

"Anahata, please take Muladhara to the chakra realm so she may heal and recover her energy. Stay beside her please" said Sahasrara.

"Yes sister" said Anahata. She went over and used her powers to levitate Muladhara off of the ground. She walked over to her tree and both of them vanished inside of it.

Master Net turned and looked up at Sahasrara.

"So...where do we go from here?" asked Net

Sahasrara turned and looked at the master. As the Crown chakra and leader of the seven sisters...it is my duty to make sure we continue this process. I will deal with Ajna, but I will carry on her training and test with Virgil from here on out" said Sahasrara.

"Understood" said Net "May we give the boy some time to heal?" he asked

"Indeed, I will return back in three days to begin his third eye training" said Sahasrara as she walked over to Ajna. She placed her hand on the triangle seal and both of them vanished.

Master Net looked down at Virgil and slowly tried to pick him up.

"I'm getting to old to lift like this" said Master Net

As he began to carry Virgil, Master Aynu was walking towards them.

"I told the boy to not run into the forest. I felt something was happening. Is he alright?" asked Aynu

"He should be fine my friend, let's get him to the hut" said Net

Both masters carried Virgil into the hut and laid him in the center next to the water hole.

Master net walked over to a table and grabbed a breathing mask, a large rope and goggles. He went over to Virgil, wrapped the rope around his waist, put both the mask and goggles on his face, making sure they were secured.

"Master Aynu, go and hook this cord to that breathing machine over there" said Master Net

Master Aynu took the cord and hooked it up to the machine. Master Net slowly lifted Virgil and placed him inside of the water. Master Aynu turned on the breathing machine and walked bac over to Master Net.

"The water should speed up his healing and help his energy return to his body" said Master Net

Both watched as Virgil began to sink to the bottom of the water hole.

As Virgil sank deeper into the water his mind sent him into a deep sleep.

Virgil awoke in his dream, again laying in front of his tree.

"How did I get here again?" asked Virgil

"Well let's see…you tried to fight one of the chakra sisters and it didn't end to well. Hehehehe" said shadow Virgil

Virgil looked up and saw his shadow version laying on one of the large tree branches.

"You're going to be in here for awhile until your body heals. Lets have some fun" said shadow Virgil as he hopped down from the tree.

"Fun? What kind of fun?" asked Virgil

Shadow Virgil turned towards the tree and placed his hand on it.

"Kun, Ura, Da, Eus, Lini " said dark Virgil

An opening formed in the center of the tree, big enough for both Virgils to walk through. Shadow Virgil turned and looked at the other Virgil. "Come…they're expecting you…Hehehehe this shall be fun"

Shadow Virgil walked through the opening and into the tree.

Virgil stood to his feet and sighed. He proceeded to walk into the opening and a strong energy ran up his spine as he entered. "What was that?" Virgil thought to himself.

He followed behind shadow Virgil down a long tunnel. The wall was filled with hieroglyphics and images of a certain person. The two continued walking down the long tunnel until they came to a giant sealed door. At the top of the door were five bright lights shining representing the chakras that Virgil already had begun to open. Coiling around them, rising to the top, was the image of what seemed to be twin snakes. "What is this?" asked Virgil

Shadow Virgil smiled "You're about to find out."

Shadow Virgil knocked on the giant door but there was no answer.

"I guess I'll have to do this my way" said Shadow Virgil as he kicked open the giant doors.

"Who daresss disssturbsss our ssslumber?"

hissed two voices from within the room.

"If you two would have opened the door, I wouldn't have disturbed you" said Shadow Virgil. He turned around and looked at the other Virgil "Come on in."

Shadow Virgil proceeded into the large chamber. Virgil followed along behind him. The chamber was filled gems and crystals of all kind. Each representing one of the seven chakras. At the far end of the chamber there was a large golden throne chair, with a large staff right next to it and above the throne there was a saying left in ancient language that translated saying "The Kings Chamber".

"What do we have here sssissster? I do not know brother, he ssseemsss very familiar" hissed the two voices.

Virgil looked around the chamber but saw nothing there. He slowly looked up above him and staring back at him were two giant cobra snakes, wrapped around the ceiling chamber. The two cobras slithered down from the ceiling to the chamber floors and surrounded Virgil.

"Ahhh, yesss. We do know you. We have been

expecting you boy" said the two cobras.

Fear began to creep into Virgils body. The snakes continued to slither around him over and over. "Hehehe, sssissssterr, he's afraid of usss" said the male cobra

"Oh, isss that ssso?" said the female cobra. They both got closer to Virgil and gave him nowhere to run. "Do you know who we are?" asked the male cobra

"Nn..no, I do not" said Virgil

"Ahhh, Sssissster, he dosssen't even know our name" said the male cobra "tsssk, tsssk, tsssk, sssuch ignorance" said thefemale cobra

The two cobra's slithered to the front of Virgil hissing. "We have gone by many namesss over the yearsss" said the two serpents

"I the female ssserpent am Ura"

"And I the male ssserpent am Kunda"

"But together our name isss....Naga of the Ancientsss" said both snakes

"Naga?....I've read about you...Master Net said Ancient Kemet Kings use to wear a symbol of you when.."

"When they have achieved full knowledge of ssself and activated all their chakrasss" said the serpents

"Woah...you're really real" said Virgil

"Every human hasss their own ssserpent power sssleeping inssside of them" said the male serpent

"But every human will not be able to awaken that power, until they have been chosssen" said the female serpent

"Chosen? What do you mean chosen?" asked Virgil

"Husssh sssissster!! That isss not for you to disssclose" said the male serpent

"My apologiesss, brother" said the female serpent.

The two serpents slithered around Virgil again.

"You however aren't fully ready yet, but you are almossst there" said the male serpent

"You ssstill have two more chakra'sss to open" said the female

"Unlike the tessst that you take with the chakra sssissster'sss our'sss will not be anywhere near friendly" said the male serpent

"If you cannot handle our energy, then you… die" said both serpents

"Hehehehe" laughed dark Virgil "You two underestimate me, he'll be ready"

The male serpent slithered over to dark Virgil

"How do you know thisss?" asked the serpent

Dark Virgil walked up to the male serpent and stared back into it's serpent eyes

"Because he'll have me this time" said Dark Virgil

The snakes hissed and laughed "You?! You've been trapped and sssleeping in here jussst asss we have. You won't make any difference boy" said the serpents

"I will make sure that he sits on that throne" said Dark Virgil.

"How about a wager?" asked the female serpent

"Wager?" asked Virgil

"Yesss, a wager. If you passs our tessst, not only will we activate your serpent energy but we will also activate your other gifts and abilities sealed inside of you as well. Now if you fail our tessst, we will take over your body and your soul will stay here, in this chamber, asssleep for thousssandsss of yearsss" said the female serpent

"Sssisster enough!" shouted the male serpent

"Husssh brother....I have thiss" said thee female serpent

"Ssso, what do you sssay my dear boy? Do we have a deal?" asked the female serpent

Virgil looked back at Dark Virgil and back up at th female serpent

"Yes, we have deal" said Virgil

Both snakes looked at each other and smiled.

"Then it's a deal" said the female serpent as she open her mouth and attacked Virgil

"Ahhh" screamed Virgil as he woke up from his dream. Breathing rapidly and checking his body making sure he was still alive. He saw that he had been resting in a hammock in one of Master Nets rooms inside the hut.

"You finally woke up" said Master Net

Virgil turned to his left and saw Master Net sitting in a chair next to the hammock

"Master Net...how..how long have I've been asleep?" asked Virgil

"Two days, I was able to speed up your recovery using a form of water therapy with the help of the water hole in the hut. How do you feel?" asked Master Net

Virgil turned and slowly started to get out of the hammock.

"I feel great...really great actually" said Virgil

"Good...I was really worried about you my boy" said Master Net "Do you remember what happened?"

Virgil looked up at Master Net "Ajna...I remember Ajna attacking Muladhara. I ran in to protect her but was of no help" said Virgil

Master Net sighed "That was foolish of you Virgil. Although you have been training with the other sister's, you were nowhere near ready to take on someone such as Ajna. Remember the seven chakra sisters are still pure cosmic energy. Your body could have been crushed in seconds going up against her"

"But wait...there's more" said Virgil "I...I remember something else, but I can't quite go into detail on how it all happened"

Master Net looked ag Virgil, confused at statement.

"There was a moment...where I lost control of my body. It was as if someone else was in control. Ajna tried to attack me but none of her attacks were working. She had fear in her eyes. I turned and somehow was able to send energy to Anahata from my body...Then I went back to sleep" said Virgil

Master Net walked to Virgil and placed a hand on his shoulder.

"An amazing thing just happened to you my boy, but it's not for me to say. You'll soon know the truth" said Master Net

"Yes master" said Virgil

The two of them began to walk to the outside of the hut, and back into the forest.

"Oh, there's one more thing Master Net. When I was asleep, I met Kundalini and Uraeus, well Naga to be exact" said Virgil

"You've already met Naga?!" said Master Net

"Yea, Dark Virgil took me to them while I was sleep"

"Who?" asked Master Net

"Oh, Dark Virgil. I met him in the Void of Darkness. Remember I told you about him" said Virgil

Master Net was just shocked. His student was growing more and more each day. All the training he had been doing was truly paying off.

The two continued to walk until they reached the front of the forest where Master Aynu was waiting for them.

"Ahh, you're awake Virgil. How are you feeling" asked Master Net

"I'm feeling better, much better" said Virgil

"Good!" said Master Net as he smacked Virgil upside his head

"Oww! What was that for?!" shouted Virgil

"If you ever run off and disobey me again, I'll kill you myself!! What were you thinking?! Trying to take on a divine being such as Ajna! Foolish! FOOLISH!!" said Master Aynu

"I was just trying to help, much apologies Master" said Virgil

"Hmph, tomorrow you will have an intensive training session to make up for your foolishness, but for now we drink tea and prepare your mind for your next test" said Master Aynu

"Understood Master, thank you" said Virgil

The three of them sat down, at a table at Aynus restaurant, and enjoyed a cup of ginseng tea. Virgil turned, looked at the cherry blossom tree and saw that Kema had returned. She was sleeping on top of the tree but felt the presence of Virgil looking at her and she awoke. She jumped down, ran over to him and laid in his lap.

"It's good to see you too Kema" said Virgil

The sun slowly began to set, and Virgil made his way home along with Kema. When he arrived home, he saw that his cousin Cole wasn't there or anywhere to be found, so he decided to take advantage of the apartment and sit in silence in the living room. He turned off all the lights and laid down on the couch. He laid there for a long time and all he could think about were the recent events that had happened to him. From entering the Void of Darkness, then attempting to take on Ajna and finally being introduced to Naga (Kundalini and Uraeus). So much was happening to him, but he was beginning to get excited. For the first time in a long time, his life was becoming exciting. It was no longer was boring or just average. He felt that he finally had begun moving in a direction that brought him happiness and understanding of who he was. Knowing he only had two more tests made him anxiously excited for many things about him were going to be revealed and that alone brought a smile to his face. The test to open his third eye was coming up, so he closed his eyes, relaxed his body and removed all negativity from his mind. He said a quick prayer to show gratitude towards his life and afterwards he went to sleep. "Thank you" he whispered.

PT. 2

THE THIRD EYE

"Virgil...Virgil...Wake up Virgil" said a woman's voice

Virgil slowly opened his eyes as the sun began to shine through the apartment window. He sat up from the couch to find a woman sitting in front of him. This woman was tall, she had beautiful melanated skin and was dressed in a beautiful purple Egyptian like outfit similar to that of a queen. Her eyes were purple, and her hair was black, long, kinky and curly. Staring at her was like staring into the universe. "You're finally awake mister Virgil" said the woman

"Who…Who are you exactly? And how did you get in here?...You know what, disregard that last question" said Virgil

"Hmmm, even though I have taken the form of an old human I use to be, I will always carry the name… Sahasrara of the crown chakra. It's nice to meet you alone and face to face Virgil" said Sahasrara

"Sahasrara…wha…what are you doing here?" he asked

"Come, gather your things. We have much to discuss" said Sahasrara

She stood to her feet and proceeded to the door "I shall wait for you outside, be quick" she said as she opened the door and exited the apartment.

Virgil quickly put his sandals on and ran outside behind her. Sahasrara was standing outside in the sun, basking in its warmth. Virgil walked up to her and stood next to her.

"I first want to say that I apologize for the events that recently happened with Ajna. As of right now she is being held in our realm where she will stand trial among the rest of us. She must face a consequence for her actions" said Sahasrara

"It's fine, no hard feelings...So because she's there...what happens now?" asked Virgil

"Hmph...well because she is unable to stand as the Third Eye Chakra guardian at the moment.... I will have to stand in her place" said Sahasrara

"I see" said Virgil

"You know...you have really impressed me Virgil" said Sahasrara

"I have? What have I done?" he asked

Sahasrara looked at Virgil and smiled

"Come, follow me" she said

She began walking to the open grassy area behind the apartments. In the back there was a random tree, all by itself, standing tall in the sun.

"Where did that tree come from?" asked Virgil

Sahasrara walked up to the tree and whispered to it "Aah, Aum, Ham, Yam, Ram, Vam, Lam" the tree began to glow and a door appeared in the center of it.

"This way" said Sahasrara as she opened the

door and proceeded into the tree. Virgil followed Sahasrara and the door, along with the tree, disappeared afterwards.

Virgil entered into a giant room and with an enormous tree in the center.

"Welcome, to the home of the seven chakra sisters" said Sahasrara

The room was filled with crystals of all sorts. Plants of all kinds spread throughout the room. There was a large fire pit in the center, in front of the tree. A water stream flowed around the center with crystals forming around it. Above their heads tiny versions of planets and clouds covered the ceiling room. Sahasrara walked to the center of the room and brought forth a sitting area, made of clouds, near the firepit.

"Virgil do come sit with me" said Sahasrara.

Virgil walked over and sat on one of the clouds.

Sahasrara summoned a flame from the fire pit, along with a table floating right beside them. On the table were two cups and a strange substance inside.

"As I was saying before, you've really impressed me Virgil. I've been watching you from the start, since you accepted Master Net's offer. You've trained and passed all of your chakra tests. You've been able to enter into the void of darkness, found in every human, and returned. You even tried to take on my sister Ajna...which failed...but I still commend you...Now you've reached the next level in your growth. Tell me...what's going through your mind right now?" asked Sahasrara

Virgil looked at Sahasrara and then began to look into the firepit.

"This all began with me seeking therapy on my life. I felt like I was losing control. From losing my ex girlfriend, to being at a job I dislike, to dealing with anger and being an overly sensitive person, and finally just wanting to be done with everything. Running into Master Net that day and then meeting him at Master Aynus restaurant...really brought the change I had been searching for my whole life. Now...I just want to see how it all ends or well how it all begins. I'm ready for a new start....a new beginning" said Virgil

"Interesting" said Sahasrara "What type of new start are you seeking from all of this?" she asked

Virgil looked up at the tiny planets floating in

the ceiling and took in a deep sigh. "I want to start following the path that will lead me to knowing more about me, and helping others like me. This journey…it has really opened my eyes" said Virgil

Sahasrara smiled and picked up the two cups, sitting on the table.

"Excellent…well, let us not waste any more time Virgil" said Sahasrara as she handed him one of the cups

"This is a substance that all must drink when going through the test to open ones third eye. Here, in our realm, we call it Mother's Nectar. It comes right from the cosmic tree of life. Every divine realm has this tree. It was a gift, many eons ago, from the divine realm called the Akashic Records. It allows those worthy of knowledge and understanding to look within themselves to have an understanding of not only themselves but the universe as well. Drinking this will take you to a place deep within you that will not only test you mentally but emotionally as well. You will see things many humans just aren't ready to see yet. The Third Eye Chakra test is a test of truth and seeing the truth for what it is. Will you accept it and grow? Or go mad with forbidden knowledge?" asked Sahasrara

Virgil took a deep breath and looked into the cup. He knew there was no turning back and that this was something he had to do. He brought the cup to his mouth and began to drink the substance. To his surprise it was actually very sweet and before he knew it his cup was empty.

"Hmph, it's all gone" said Virgil

He looked over at Sahasrara as she grinned at him mysteriously. He saw that she had yet to take a sip of her drink.

"Are you not going to drink yours?" he asked

She laughed as she took a sip "Oh Virgil, this here cup is nothing more than Master Aynu and Nets favorite ginseng tea"

Virgil's mouth dropped as he watched Sahasrara take another sip of her tea.

"Mmm, that reminds me, the effects of Mother's Nectar should be taking effect right...now"

"What are you..." said Virgil as he froze in mid sentence.

Virgil's body had become completely still. He

couldn't feel or move his feet, legs, arms, fingers or anything for that matter. All he could do was listen to his thoughts and watch what was happening in front of him.

"What kind of drink did she give me?! I can't feel anything!" said Virgil in his mind.

"Mother's Nectar is a very strong substance. It will automatically cleanse all of your chakras and open them up. It will clean, detoxify and alkalize the entire human body as well. During this process, however, your body will be in a state of temporary paralysis state. The only time you will move is when the body is ready to purge itself of anything negative inside of you.

"Purge?! What do you mean" said Virgil as his body began to feel nauseous.

"Ah, for example, the mother is now in control of your body" said Sahasrara as she levitated a small crystal pot onto Virgil's lap.

Virgil's body slightly leaned over the pot and he began to spew out a black liquid substance.

His body sat back up and froze again.

"What just happened, how am I not controlling

my body?!" he asked himself

"As I said before, the mother is in control and while she does her work, we shall begin your third eye chakra test" said Sahasrara as she snapped her fingers three times.

The room went dark and the only thing left visible was the fire coming from the firepit.

Virgil's body slowly turned towards it and his eyes were locked onto the fire.

The fire began to fade in and out, as well as change to many different colors. It was as if it was trying to talk to him.

"Let me tell you a story Virgil" said Sahasrara voice from afar.

"Long ago, in the void of space, there was a star. A very beautiful, bright, tiny star filled with nothing but star dust. This star was one of many millions other stars floating in the cosmos. Where did these stars come from? No one truly knows, but one day this particular star ventured off deep into the void of space. It came across a being known as a galaxy. When the star saw the galaxy, it saw that the galaxy was doing something special. It was experiencing a phenomena called life. There were multiple stars and planets within the galaxy all experiencing this amazing thing. The little star floated over to the galaxy and inside the center it found the star creating this entire galaxy. It went over and asked "how are you doing this? And how can I experience it?" The star creating the galaxy looked at the other tiny star and said…"All it takes is a thought". The tiny star looked confused as the other star floated away from it along with it's galaxy. "A thought" the tiny star said, "but how do I do that?" it asked, but it was too late. The other star had already traveled too far. The tiny star continued to wander around in the dark space. It couldn't stop thinking about what the other star said to it. "All it takes it a thought?" So the little star thought of one thing…Life. Then from its inner tiny consciousness, poof, an entire mini galaxy started to form right in front of it. It was indeed small but it was the start of something much, much larger coming into existence"

The flame in front of Virgil shifted and changed throughout the entire story and then it went dark.

"Virgil…you are part of that tiny galaxies thought…you are part of that large existence…you a part of this experience called life" said Sahasrara

From the firepit a blueish purple flame appeared and from that flame appeared a planet similar to earth.

"In this galaxy, in this reality there was an ancient being who discovered seven principles that help to govern the laws of this universe. That being went by many names but the one name he is truly known by is the name Thoth. Thoth was an ancient Kemite (Egyptian) who was known as a master of masters and indeed he was. His knowledge and mind were untouched by those back in his time. He discovered that in this world there were seven principles that govern over everything here in this life. The beings existing in this galaxy must understand this in order to understand the true picture of life. The first principle is the Law of Mentalism, which means that The Universe is Mental. The All is Mind. The second principle is The Law of Correspondence, which means As Above, so Below; As Below, So Above. The third principle is The Law of Vibration, which means nothing is every resting, everything moves and everything vibrates. The fourth principle is the Law of Polarity, which means everything is dual; everything has poles and everything has it's pair of opposites. The fifth principle is the Law of Rhythm, which means everything flows, everything has its tides, all things rise and all things fall. The sixth principle is the Law of Cause and Effect, which means for every cause there will be an effect, and every effect has its cause, everything happens according to the universe las. Finally the seventh principle, the Law of Gender, which states that everything has a gender. The Masculine and Feminine energy manifest on all planes. These seven principles govern over the law of this reality and it's existence" said Sahasrara

The flame began to grow and soon was the size of a human. The heat from the flame began to warm Virgil's body. His body leaned over the crystal pot again and he spewed more dark liquid from his body. His body sat back up and his eyes recentered into the flame.

"Now that you know of the seven principles, I will now teach you how to feel and understand these principles in the universe. Doing this will allow your third eye to see more of the world for what it is and what it isn't" said Sahasrara "Now mother, stand the boy's body up and slowly walk him into the flame"

Virgils body slowly stood up "What are you doing?" he asked himself

It slowly began to walk towards the flame "Stop! Stop! You'll kill me! Stop!" he shouted in his mind but his body continued to walk. The flame began to rise again and a hand slowly reached out towards Virgil. "Come" said the flame.

Virgil's hand reached out towards the flame and it grabbed the hand coming from the flame. The hand slowly pulled Virgils body into the flame "Noooooo! Stop enough!" said Virgil in his mind but it was too late, his body was now engulfed in the flame.

The flames covered Virgil's body and burnt all of his clothes but they did not burn him. The heat from the flame grew hotter but Virgil felt no pain, and his body received no burns from it either.

"The flame has chosen to show you the truth Virgil…do you accept?" asked Sahasrara

Virgils head slowly nodded and his eyes closed.

"Virgil…to understand this chakra…you have to understand the meaning of balance. The Third Eye reveals to us things that can either feed us love or cause us pain. When there is light…there is darkness…where there is peace…there is chaos… where there is masculine energy…there is feminine energy…where there is life…there is death…there is always a balance" said Sahsarara

Virgil, still with his eyes closed, saw the sun. From the sun he saw the planets and from the planets he saw his galaxy. His mind took him to the center of the galaxy and there in the middle was a tiny star, similar to that of the sun. The star was sending out large vibrational waves that traveled through the entire galaxy. Virgil was pulled closer and closer to the star until he could feel every wave moving through him.

"What is this I am feeling" he asked

The star began to push more and more vibrations out.

"What you're feeling…is love, Virgil. Love beyond anything or any human could every comprehend. This stars love for all things in this galaxy is so strong, because it is finally experiencing life. The being that created this star placed loved inside of it more than any other feeling and it does the same for everything else in it's galaxy" said

Sahasrara

Virgil looked deeper at the star and say there were little dust particles floating inside but there was something else. It was as if there was a reflection coming from inside of the star. Virgil saw that inside of the star was another version of him, staring right back at him smiling. "All this time...it's been me" said Virgil

The flames from the firepit began to subside and lower down. Virgil was standing there with no clothes on, staring into the darkness. The effects of Mother's Nectar were beginning to wear off and he was now in control of his body. A light began to emit from behind him and it was the divine tree. The tree shot a beam of light at Virgil and new garments of clothes appeared on him. The divine tree lowered one of its branches down to Virgil and hanging from it was an indigo lotus flower. Virgil grabbed the lotus flower from the branch and placed it near his forehead. "I understand now" said Virgil

"Congratulations Virgil...you've passed" said Sahasrara "Preparations have already been made for your final test. Master Net and the others await for you in the sacred forest. I will be seeing you in Kemet in three weeks" said Sahasrara

"Kemet?" asked Virgil

"Yes…your final test shall be taken in Kemet, also known as Egypt. I shall await for you there young Virgil and we shall finally bring your journey to an amazing…beginning" said Sahasrara

She opened a portal that led back to the sacred forest and before leaving she grabbed Virgils hand.

"May the spirit and source of all things guide you to a path of happiness, love and inner peace." She hugged him and sent him on his way. Virgil walked through the portal and was back in the sacred forest standing in front of Ajnas tree. He held the indigo lotus flower in his hand and began to walk towards Master Nets hut. Waiting for him, on the outside, was Master Net, Master Aynu and Kema.

"You've returned I see" said Master Aynu

"How did the test go?" asked Master Net

Virgil looked at the lotus flower and back up at his master "It went perfect" said Virgil

Master Net handed Virgil a cup of tea "three weeks...Egypt...are you ready?" asked Master Net

Virgil took a sip and gazed into the sun as it was setting over the forest.

"Yeah...I'm ready"

CHAPTER 7

THE MASTER AND THE APPRENTICE

Twelve long months had passed since the beginning of Virgil's journey. It started off by running into a strange old man while leaving his counseling session. The old man offered him an escape and truth that turned into something bigger. A journey to self-discovery, self-love and inner peace. Even though he was grateful for being on this journey he still could not put his finger on the reason of why he was chosen. Why did Master Net choose him, why did Master Aynu decided to train him. Why were the chakra sister's so eager to help him learn about himself and heal his past? Why was he important? So many questions had little to no answers. Little did he know, all of the questions would soon be answered.

Master Net, Master Aynu, Kema and Virgil were now all on a plane heading to Egypt. After being told by the white spirit to go there, Virgil didn't hesitate. Not knowing how long he would be gone, he decided it was time to let go of his job at the school system and say goodbye to his students but knew he would see them one day again. He took all of his money out of his bank account and savings. He gave some of it to his sisters and most of it to his cousin Cole. It was enough to pay for rent and other bills in the apartment for the next two months. He gave his cousin a hug and told him that he would be back one day, but he didn't know when. Cole understood and gave him reassurance that home would still be there when he returned. Master Net had already made arrangements for their flight and they all began their journey to Egypt for their final chapter but new beginning.

The plane trip to Egypt didn't last too long. Master Net and Master Aynu both knew many people with their own private jets and were more than welcome to help them get to their destination.

Virgil spent most of his time looking out the window and petting Kema while she slept on him. Both Master's spent most of their time playing several games of chess and drinking many cups of tea. In no time, they arrived in a private section at the Cairo International Airport in Egypt.

"Ahhh finally we arrived. I despise these airplanes" said Master Aynu.

"Old friend, we've been flying for years. You should be accustomed to them now" said Master Net

"NEVER! Keep me on the ground" said Master Aynu

Virgil chuckled and followed his Masters out of the plane.

Waiting outside the plane and standing next to a black SUV was Brya (Muladhara).

"Virgil!!" shouted Brya as she ran to him and gave him a hug!

Virgil and Brya hugged each other for a few moments before separating "Thank you for what you did awhile ago with Ajna. I never had a chance to tell you that" said Brya

Virgil smiled and put his hand on his head "It was nothing, trust me. I was in the way anyway" said Virgil I'm so proud of you" said Brya "I can tell you've grown so much! I could feel your energy coming from the plane."

"Thank you Brya, this has been a very interesting year...but I'm happy about where I am now...Thank you for helping me in the beginning. You really started my journey off right" said Virgil

"That's my duty Virgil...now let's get you and the others to your camp site"

"CAMP SITE!!!" yelled Virgil

He turned and looked at the Masters "You two said we were staying in a hotel!"

Both Master Net and Aynu looked at each other

"Did you say that? Because I didn't" said Master Aynu

"I have no idea what he's talking about" said Master Net

Both Master's walked towards the SUV and hopped in. Virgil looked down at Kema, standing beside him and Kema looked up at Virgil. Both released sigh and hopped into the SUV.

"So where is this camp site?" asked Virgil

"It's right on the outskirts of town, with a beautiful view of the Giza Pyramids" said Brya

"My sisters are all their waiting on you all to get there"

"Ahhhh, so the others finally decided to take on a human form" said Master Net

"Just for this occasion, this will be an event to remember" said Brya as she cranked the car and began to drive off.

As they traveled through the city, a strange feeling began to take over Virgil. Even though it was his first in Egypt, he felt like he had been there before. He couldn't explain it, but it felt like he had returned home.

They had arrived to an outpost not too far out from the city.

"This is where we exit guys!" said Brya

Everyone exited the SUV and waiting for them at the outpost were four camels.

"Alright, these camels will get us the rest of the way" said Brya

Virgil looked at the camels and then back at the SUV

"Exactly why are we riding camels when we have a fully functioning car?" he asked

Brya laughed "Because there's nothing like a camel ride through the desert. Make sure you guys wrap up. It's going to be a long and sunny ride through the desert"

Everyone hopped on their camel while Virgil struggled to get on his.

"This guy doesn't like me!" yelled Virgil

"Virgil, Virgil, Virgil…you have to be gentle my friend" said Master Net

With a sigh Virgil calmy looked at the camel, greeting it and asking for permission to ride. The camel lowered itself down, acknowledging Virgils request.

Master Net smiled and nodded his head. Kema hopped on the same camel as Virgil and the group set off into the hot desert.

The blazing sun beamed down onto the desert, and heat began to rise. Master Net looked behind and saw that Virgil was having. Was having a difficult time with the sun. He laughed and slowed his camel down. "Aynu and Brya, you two go on ahead. I need to talk to Virgil"

The two nodded and continued on ahead. Master Net Wait for Virgils camel to catch up, as Virgil laid on it suffering from the heat. "You know, I use to always say Georgia has the worst heat...I take it all back now" said Virgil

Master Net laughed "It isn't that bad, all those days meditating in the sun should have helped you prepare for this"

Virgil looked up at the sun and back at Master Net "Nah...I wasn't prepared" said Virgil. "So...where exactly are we riding to? I thought we were staying in a hotel?" asked Virgil

"For this occasion, it would be foolish to stay inside" said Master Net

The two continued to ride far behind the others. Master Net reached into a bag, on the side of his camel and pulled out a small bag. He turned towards Virgil and handed him the bag.

"This is for you...I've waited since the day we met to give you this" said Master Net

Virgil grabbed the bag, loosened the string on the side and pulled out two items. First was a small black crystal necklace wrapped in copper, carved with Egyptian hieroglyphics on it. The second was a black pyramid that had the seven chakras lined up from top to bottom starting with the root chakra all the way to the crown chakra. Wrapped around the pyramid was a shiny cobra made out of pure copper.

"Wow...what is this for?" asked Virgil

"When we first met, you asked me about my necklace and wanted one of your own. Those two items are made specially for you by me, to see you through your final test" said Master Net.

Virgil held both items in his hand as the light form the sun shined down upon them.

"Ahh, do you feel it Virgil...the sun is blessing the crystals with it's energy...everything is coming together my young apprentice" said Master Net

Virgil placed the pyramid in his robe pocket and

put the necklace on around his neck.

"Master Net...Thank you...this means a lot" said Virgil

"Don't thank me Virgil, you've earned it...You've come a long way since I ran into you leaving your therapist. You have become everything I knew you were meant to become, and there is so much more coming your way my boy" said Master Net

Virgil looked at Master Net and for the first time he could see a gold aura covering his body and emitting a strong amount of energy.

"Master Net..."

"I know Virgil...I owe you a lot of answers... and now I shall finally tell you everything" said Master Net

"To start off...I want to properly reintroduce myself...to you I am Master Net, to the universe my name is Neteru Master Naqi. I am a being that has roamed this amazing planet for over three thousand years. I was born here...in the Nubian place you call Egypt. I call myself a Neteru because I have taken the time to not only know myself, but I know and have obtain the secret power of spirit, life, death and the universe. The ancient ancestral spirit that I am linked with… is none of than the master of master's himself…Thoth"

"Thoth!!" shouted Virgil "You…You are connected with Thoth! Wait…you've been alive for three thousand years?! How?!?" said Virgil

Master Net chuckled "Yes I am, he and his Queen Ma'at, have been preparing for this generation of Neteru to rise. You will become one of many Neteru… very soon but shhh, let me finish my story first Virgil. Now where was I…Ahhh that's right…I was born in Egypt, but I prefer to call it Kemet. Now to you, three thousand seems like a long time, but when you know the things I know and have studied, life, death, the stars and the cosmos…it's not that long" said Master Net.

"I was born to an amazing mother and father. We lived on the outskirts of Kemet and would you believe there was actual live vegetation in those days. My mother was a master of knowing nature and how to take care of it. My father was wise in the art of knowledge and a strong warrior for his land…Ahh…I can still remember their faces as if it was yesterday. Amazing, strong, wise and loving they were. I tell you my dear boy, melanated people were beyond amazing in those times" said Master Net as he smiled and shed a tear.

"What happened…" asked Virgil

"My parents… were taken away from me when I was only just a small boy. Our home was destroyed… you see in those days, just like in the days we live in now, many people did not like us…They were jealous of our wisdom, our strength, our land, our love, and our connection to the universe. We let our guard down for one split second…and just like that…we lost our power, our land and even our history. Betrayed by many, even by some that looked like us. My father lost his life in combat and my mother was taken as a prisoner. Before I could get captured my mother hid me deep within the forest not too far from our home. She asked nature and the spirits to protect me as she placed me in a small hole under a tree…I never saw her of my father ever again after that day. I lived alone for many months and as a child, that is terrifying. Walking the land and scavenging for food, not knowing if I would lose my life as well…but Mother Gaia…this planet, she listened to my mother and protected me. She led me to a person who would one day change my life".

"Who was that?" asked Virgil

"Will you let me finish!" said Master Net as he laughed.

"One day I was out looking for food and I then came across a man, sitting underneath a tree. He had a bountiful amount of fruit and vegetables with him. He was very old so I knew if I could run and snatch of few things, he couldn't catch me...but oh boy was I wrong. He didn't see me from the direction I was coming, I ran up, took a handful of fruits and vegetables, and took off running. The old man turned around, and just sat there looking at me as I ran off with as much food as I could. I ran and ran, throughout the forest until I thought I had reached a good amount of distance between the two of us. I sat down and started to feed myself. All of a sudden, I heard someone say, "you dropped this back there." I looked up and in front of me was old man. I was shocked because I knew for a fact, he wasn't capable of catching up to me...he was too old.

"If you're going to steal, try not to drop

anything. These fruits are very valuable my boy" he said to me. I stood there in awe and I asked him "How? How did you find me or even catch up to me?"

He laughed at me, then sat next to me and started to eat the fruit.

"May I join you?" he asked

Still shook I sat next to him and began to eat. The man posed no threat to me nor did I sense any hostility from him. We sat there, ate for a while and enjoyed the peaceful sounds of nature.

The man turned and looked at me "What is your name boy?" he asked

I looked at him and said "Naqi"

The old man nodded "Hmmm, interesting" he said "Your parents...they were taken from you, weren't they?" he asked

I looked down, nodded my head and began to cry.

The old man patted my head "No need to cry my boy..." said the old man

"How would you like to go on a journey with

me throughout this land? This land has become dangerous and you shouldn't be wandering this forest alone" he said

I looked at him and at first, I was hesitant. Then deep inside my mind, I heard my mothers voice "Go my son" she said. I nodded and accepted his offer. Virgil… that was the best decision, till this day, of my life" said Master Net

Master Net looked at Virgil "That was the beginning of my journey…that you're taking now. I, however, was much younger than you but that old man showed me things that no other man or being could ever show me when it comes to this universe"

"What was his name" asked Virgil

Master Net looked up into the sky "Anu… Master Anu…he was being so in tune with the cosmos, the universe, time, reality, the spirit and that life that lives inside of us all… it seemed unreal" said Master Net

"What happened to him?" asked Virgil

Master Net sighed and chuckled "He fulfilled one of his many purposes…"

"His many purposes?" asked Virgil

"Yes...you see Virgil...we all have a path and purpose. Some, during this life, are aware of it and some go many years never knowing it. Master Anu was aware of his purpose way before he ever ran into me. He knew his purpose was to pass on all of his teachings, wisdom, knowledge and love to me...so that one day...I may pass it all on to you" said Master Net

Virgil looked at Master Net confused "To me? ...Why me?" asked Virgil

Master Net chuckled "Virgil...you have no idea how important you are to an even greater puzzle in this universe" said Master Net

"To answer one of your many questions...I've known about you since the day my Master journeyed off back into the spirit realm"

"...what?" asked Virgil "You've...you've known about me for"

"Over thousands of years...yes...I remember when I found out...Master Anu and I we were on the Abu Galoum beach in Dahab. At that time we called it the gateway to the heavens because when night falls, it's beyond beautiful. It's like looking into heaven. Master Anu took me there after I had been learning and training with him for the last several years. What I thought to be a peaceful day of relaxation… turned out to be one of the hardest days of my life. On that day…in order for me to achieve my purpose in growing into the man and being you see today…I had to let my master go and learn to be alone in this world. The final and true test for any being in this world, is learning to be alone with self, so that true inner work and healing can take place. I didn't understand it at first nor did I care to understand at that time. When night came…I looked at Master Anu…I saw his spirit leave his body that day. My master's spirit was mighty, strong and so very humble. You would have thought it wasn't of this world. His body, this vessel, it turned into ash and was carried off into the ocean by the wind…all that was left of him was his garments. I picked them up and as I did the moon shined down upon me. I looked up at the moon and stared into its beauty. Then the words of my master came to me…Death is never the end…but the beginning. On that day is when I began my process to becoming a Neteru. That is also when I turned around on the beach to see two women standing not too far behind me…It was Anahata and Ma'at.

Ma'at had tasked Anahata to be my guide and protector for the next three thousand years...even though she had a duty as one of the seven chakra sisters. On that day that is when I learned of you. I know more about you than you know about yourself...but that is not my business to tell. It is for you to find out very soon" said Master Net "You spirit has been on this planet for years Virgil...waiting for the right time to awaken. Like I've told you, you've lived many lives...but this life you live now...will be your most important one yet" said Master Net

Virgil looked at Master Net in awe and couldn't quite process all he had just heard.

"Soon...all will be revealed...my young apprentice" said Master Net.

As the two continued to ride along they saw that they were getting closer to their destination. Master Aynu and Brya had stopped in the middle of the desert next to what seemed to be a small hand statue holding a crystal ball. Once Virgil and Master Net arrived at the statue they hopped off their camels and walked up towards the others.

"What is this?" asked Virgil

"This…is a veil key" said Brya "It only reveals itself to those worthy of traversing between different worlds on this earth"

"Different…worlds?" asked Virgil

Brya turned and looked at Master Net "You haven't taught him of the other realms yet?" she asked

"That is something he will discover soon on his own…for now I want his eyes to see and observe" said Master Net

Brya nodded and placed her hand on the crystal ball.

"I Muladhara of the Seven Sister's request access into the Oasis Haven Realm"

The crystal ball began to glow and a small portal appeared in front of them. A calm breeze came through the portal and the smell of fresh water along with it. Brya and Master Aynu walked through the portal, along with Kema. Master Net looked at Virgil, and signaled him to come. Master Net walked through and Virgil slowly followed. What was waiting for them on the other side was unimaginably amazing.

Virgil stepped out on the other side of the portal and a beam of light from the sun came shining down upon him. Virgil looked around and saw that they were in an Oasis in the desert but it wasn't normal or how the internet described one at least. This Oasis was majestic, and completely other worldly. The trees were tall and greener than normal. The air was fresh and with every breath it brought life to Virgil. The large body of water in the center was crystal clear and beaming its bright light from the sky was the sun...or at least that's what Virgil thought. Virgil looked up in the sky and couldn't believe his eyes. The sun wasn't what was shining down on him, but it was a completely different star. This star was orange and had a bright green hue surrounding it. This star created an entirely different environment. The sky was covered with a purple aura and you could see many other stars in the sky as well. The star began to emit and large amount of heat onto the surface, but the heat felt amazing. It was like living on a new planet and it felt amazing. Then there right on the other side of the oasis was a massive golden pyramid.

"Welcome to the hidden Oasis Realm. A safe haven for those journeying between the physical and spiritual world" said Master Net

"Are…are we still on earth?" asked Virgil

"Mmmmm, something like that…This is what our earth should be…Come, lets set up camp" said Master Net

"Wait…that's all you're going to say!" said Virgil as he followed Master Net.

The group walked closer to the water in the center of the oasis and began setting up large tents. Virgil was still amazed at the world he was currently observing. Never could he imagine such a place and the whole time it was right in front of him.

"It's beautiful isn't it?" said Brya

Virgil looked at her and nodded his head.

"One day, when everything has fallen into place…you earth will look like this too" she said

Virgil looked at her "Really?" he asked

She nodded "yes, but there are going to be many things to take place on your earth. Much corruption, lies, chaos, and pain is on yours. Even though those things are needed in the world, there is an unbalance on your earth….There should always be a balance...but...all that is about to change...with you" said Brya as she looked up at Virgil and then up into the sky

"Master Net still hasn't explained to me my purpose...there's a lot actually he hasn't explained to me" said Virgil

"All those answers you shall receive tonight and in the coming future" said Brya

"Now help me set up this last tent, we have a major ceremony to prepare for" she said

"Ceremony?" asked Virgil

The two began setting up the last tent, which was for Sahasrara for when she arrived.

On this planet, when night fall comes, the aura in the sky turns green. Similar to the aurora lights on Virgils earth.

Master Aynu was preparing a firepit in the center of the camp. On a hill, outside of camp, Master Net and Kema observed Virgil and the stars.

"He's grown so much these last few months...do you think we rushed his process? A journey like this shouldn't be rushed" said Kema

"Kema...you and I both know that this journey shouldn't be taken lightly. However, we both know that this is prophecy...Virgils journey is very different from anyone else's we've encountered because he is not just anyone. We both know his true name... and that it is already written in the stars for what he must do" said Master Net

"I understand that Net...I am one of the seven sisters you're talking too. I'm...I'm just worried about him...I've grown to love that boy...I've known about him for thousands of years and you would have thought I would have been more prepared for this. Seeing him being born over and over, watching him grow and now...he's finally here..." said Kema

"I know... I've grown to love him as literally my own in this short time...but...I need you to be ready to help Virgil when that time comes" said Master Net "Just as you have helped me"

Kema looked at Master Net

"That is not my call...but the call of Sahasrara whether I may stay beside him or not" she said

The night began to set in and the flares from the

fire began to rise into the sky. Everyone sat around the enjoying some of Master Aynu's ginseng and blue lotus tea with a small hint of molasses (it was his new mixture). Master Net turned and looked at the top of a sand dune. Walking from the sand was a stranger dressed in all black clothing, covering their face and entire body except for their eyes. The strange person approached the group, and exchanged greetings.

"Greetings travelers, and greetings to you Muladhara one of the seven chakra sisters. I am Mistress Nia, one of the guardians of the Oasis Realm. I have already spoken to madam Sahasrara, preparations for tomorrows ceremony have already been put in place. Is there anything that I may assist you with tonight?" asked the woman.

"Thank you for all that you've done sister, we should be fine tonight" said Brya (Muladhara)

The woman bowed before them and turned to look at Virgil. She locked eyes with him and walked over towards him.

"Are you Virgil?" asked the woman

Virgil nodded his head and stood to his feet.

"Ye...yes I, I, I am Virgil...I think" he said

Master Net and Master Aynu smacked their foreheads and continued to drink their tea. Brya began to giggle and shack her head.

The woman giggled herself and placed her hand onto Virgils forehead

"Still young but so much potential" said the woman "I send you blessings and may the spirit guides lead you to your truth on this journey. We shall await you on the other side" said the woman.

She removed her hand and began to walk off back into the night.

"Smooth, very smooth" said Master Net

"The boy has learned nothing" said Master Aynu

"Give him a break you two" said Brya while laughing

Virgil looked at all three of them "What? What did I do?" asked Virgil

Virgil sat down and began to enjoy the rest of his tea. Master Net leaned over and whispered, "It was the eyes, wasn't it?" he asked as he chuckled

Virgil spit his tea out "Master!!" he shouted

"Don't you dare waste my new formula tea boy! That's it time for late night training!" shouted Master Aynu

Master Net and Brya laughed as Virgil was dragged by Master Aynu to go train.

Brya looked at Master Net "You haven't told him, have you?" she asked

He shook his head "No...and I won't tell him" he said

"Why not? I think he's ready" she said

Master Net looked at Brya "We all think we're ready...until it happens" he said

A flashing light came from one of the tents "He's right Muladhara"

Out of the tent walked Sahasrara "This approach is for the best"

"Sister..." said Brya

"Virgils time has come...we begin the ceremony tonight...bring him to golden pyramid Master Net...Muladhara, come with me" said Sahasrara

"Sahasrara…now? Why not tomorrow?" asked Master Net

"It is not my call" as she looked up into the sky and back at Master Net "It is theirs" she said and began to walk to the golden pyramid.

Brya stood up, went over to hug Master net and followed behind Sahasrara.

Master Net watched them as they walked towards the pyramid. Master Net turned and walked over towards Aynu and Virgil.

"Virgil go to your tent and put on your garments you were given after your last test" said Master Net

Virgil and Aynu looked at Master Net

"Sahasrara said we are beginning the final ceremony tonight" said Master Net

"Tonght?!?!" shouted Virgil and Aynu

"Net…why now, tonight was supposed to be the night of rest" said Aynu

"I know, I know…but this isn't Sahasrara doing" said Net

Aynu looked at Net with confusion "Do you think?" asked Aynu

"I don't think…I know" said Net

Aynu nodded "Virgil…go get ready…we will wait for you at the top of that dune leading to the golden pyramid" said Aynu

Virgil sighed "okay" he began to walk to his tent.

"And put some pep in your step boy!" shouted Aynu

Virgil walked off to the tent and Master Net turned towards Aynu.

"Aynu, my friend, I need you to go on ahead. This walk to the pyramid must be with my and Virgil. Master and Apprentice" said Master Net

"Hmm, I understand my friend. I shall await you both" said Aynu

Aynu began walking towards the pyramid and while Net waited for Virgil by his tent.

Virgil walked outside of his tent dressed in his ancient garment given to him from his last test.

"Where is everyone?" he asked

Master Net walked up to Virgil and placed a hand on his shoulder.

"Come, let us walk to the pyramid. Don't forget your necklace and crystal I made for you" said Master Net

The two began walking to the pyramid, slowly.

"Virgil...what are three things you have learned since taking this journey with me?" asked Master Net

Virgil looked up at the moon, which was strangely shining orange.

"Hmmm" he thought

"Well, there are many thing's I've learned" he said

"One thing that really stands out, I've learned to let go...let go of the past and everything that has held me back all these years from just being happy with me and loving me" said Virgil

"Hmmm, so self love and self worth?" asked Master Net

"Yea, exactly that" said Virgil

"I think this is the most I've ever just loved me and who I am. I feel amazing, I feel…I feel like I actually mean something in this life. I don't feel…pointless or useless"

Master Net smiled "Good…what else?"

"Hmmm" thought Virgil

"I've also learned to tackle my demons and traumas. By that I mean…just actually look inside myself and see that I have faults and it's okay to acknowledge those faults. Doing that…I can actually begin to heal, move forward in life and grow. Yea…I can actually grow from looking within myself instead of looking in the world for the problem" said Virgil

"Ahhh, that's a really good one" said Master Net

"Lastly…learn to make every moment in my life count. Live in the present, not in the past or the future. When I live in the now, I see more of the world. I feel more of the world. I connect more….Ahhh there's so much Master Net! It's hard to just pick three!" said Virgil

Master Net laughed "And that's what makes this moment so special" he said

"This whole year, you've gone from a boy who was depressed and unhappy with his life to now seeing the bigger picture of everything. You've connected to life and by doing that you've connected with yourself. That alone...is true growth" said Master Net

Virgil chuckled "Yea...so what now?" he asked

"Now...you take on your final test...the hardest test anyone must take on this journey...but I know you are more than ready" said Master Net

Master Net and Virgil reached the top of the sand dune where they could see the giant golden pyramid for all of it's glory and beauty.

"Woah...I never thought I would be this close to a pyramid" said Virgil

On the side of the pyramid sat a smaller pyramid. Virgil turned and looked at Master Net.

"I thought there were three pyramids in Egypt?" he asked

Master Net smiled "I told you...were not on your earth anymore" he said.

Both began walking towards the pyramids were

everyone was awaiting them.

Standing in front of the larger pyramid were five of the chakra sisters. Master Aynu and Kema were standing in front of the second pyramid. Mistress Nia approached Virgil and Master Net as they began to approach the ceremonial area.

"We have been awaiting for your arrival Master Net and young Master Virgil. Please come this way" said the Mistress

Virgil smiled "She called me a young master" he said

"Hush" said Master Net

In front of the pyramid was a large fire pit. Everyone began to move towards the fire pit once Virgil and Master net had arrived.

Mistress Nia walked over to Sahasrara and bowed

"The Oasis has the protection of all the spirit guides and ancestors. You may now commence with the final ceremony" said the Mistress

"Thank you, sister," said Sahasrara

Sahasrara and the chakra sisters approached the

fire. Kema walked over and sat in between Virgil and Master Net. Master Aynu stood off to the side and watched from a distance.

"Greetings to all that are here on this final ceremonial journey of awakening. I Sahasrara of the crown chakra now call this ceremony to order"

"Asé" said all the sisters

"Neteru Master Naqi...whom do bring to us, the sisters of the divine chakras of the universe and to the ancestors of this universe?" asked Sahasrara

Master Net walked towards the fire "I Neteru Master Naqi bring forth my apprentice Young Master Virgil, future of the Neteru" said Master Net

Virgil looked at Master Net in shocked and said to himself "Future of what?!"

"Asé" said the sister's

Sahasrara motioned her hands towards Virgil "Come, young master Virgil"

Virgil, now nervous, slowly walked towards the fire.

Master Net leaned over and whispered "Let go of all fear...you are protected my apprentice" he said

Virgil, still nervous, nodded his head.

"Sisters of the seven chakras…do you approve of this young master and see that he is worthy of entering into the great pyramids of the ancients?" asked Sahasrara

"Asé" said the sister's

Sahasrara nodded "Understood"

She looked up into the sky, at the moon "Ancestors of the past…do you accept this young master and see his worth of entering into your temple of divine power, wisdom, knowledge and love?" she asked.

A ray of light shined down from the moon into the fire changing the fires color to a bright light purple. A gust of wind came over the area rising the flames of the fire to the sky, as if it was reaching for the heavens.

"Ase" said Sahasrara

Sahasrara bowed before the flame and walked over to Virgil

"Before you and I can enter into the temple

...you must look within and recite the code of the seven chakras. This code can only be recited by someone who has done the true inner work and can feel it's power inside of them. Are you prepared?" she asked?

"Ye...Yes" said Virgil

Sahasrara smiled "I know you are...step to the flame young master"

Virgil walked to the flame with Sahasrara.

"Place your hands in the prayer position, keep your back straight, head forward and eyes closed...The flame awaits you" said Sahasrara

Virgil took a deep breath, but still felt the nervous tension in his body. A small chill ran up his spine and a calming sensation overcame him. A voice, from within, spoke to him.

"Relax and repeat, out loud, after me" said the voice

"I have accepted the abundance in my life, and I am fully grounded" said the voice

"I have accepted the abundance in my life, and I am fully grounded" said Virgil

The flame of the fire turned red, showing respect to Muladhara and the root chakra.

Muladhara smiled and allowed her human self to shed a tear.

"I am open to receive all that life offers. I value and trust myself. I am calm and confident. I give love for I am love. I am guided by my inner wisdom. I am enough" said the voice.

Virgil took another deep breath and exhaled

"I am open to receive all that life offers! I value and trust myself! I am calm and confident! I give love for I am love! I am guided by my inner wisdom! I am enough!" shouted Virgil

The flame began to change colors, from orange, to yellow, to green, blue and indigo.

"I am at peace...I am balance...I am whole...I honor my body as a temple that fully nourishes my soul and spirit" said the voice

"I am at peace...I am balance...I am whole...I honor my body as a temple that fully nourishes my soul and spirit!" said Virgil

The flame slowly calmed down and in that small

second a burst of purple light rosed to the heavens from the flame.

"Open your eyes Virgil" said Sahasrara

Virgil opened his eyes and saw everyone standing in front of him.

"Asé" said everyone standing around the flame

Kema let out a calm meow and walked over towards her sisters.

"The first test is complete…now on to the next" said Sahasrara

Sahasrara looked at Master Net and nodded her head. Master Net nodded back.

"Come Virgil, let us go to the first Pyramid" said Sahasrara

Virgil and Sahasrara began walking to the smaller pyramid.

Virgil turned and looked at Master Net and the others. Muladhara smiled and whispered "Goodluck Virgil"

Virgil smiled and walked on towards the pyramid. Waiting for them on the outside were

Master Aynu and Mistress Nia. Aynu was holding a gold cup in his hand and a double pipe in the other hand.

"Before entering you must again drink a cup of mothers nectar and Master Aynu must administer the powder of the kings to you" said Sahasrara

Virgil nodded and walked towards Master Aynu.

Master Aynu bowed before Virgil and Sahasrara.

"Young Master Virgil...I Master Aynu and proud to administer the powder of the kings to you and the mother's nectar drink. Do you accept?" asked Aynu

Virgil nodded and grabbed the cup from Master Aynu.

Aynu placed the double pipe into Virgils nose and blew into it. The powder was not like the one Master Net gave Virgil along time ago. It was stronger and Virgil could feel his body beginning to shake. Sahasrara placed her hand on Virgil to relax him. Virgil took a deep breath in through his mouth and exhaled slowly.

"Well done" said Master Aynu "Now drink"

Virgil began to drink from the golden cup, and remembered that the nectar was not as bad as everything else he had done. After he had finished drinking he gave the cup back to Master Aynu and bowed. Mistress Nia turned towards the pyramid and placed her hand on it. She whispered to it and a door slowly began to appear and open in front of them.

"The pyramid of the crown chakra awaits you" said Mistress Nia

"Let us venture in" said Sahasrara

The two began to walk into the pyramid, which was very dark, but torches lit their way. The pyramid door closed once they were deep within, and Virgil knew there was no turning back from here.

PT. 2

THE AWAKENING

Deeper into the pyramid Virgil and Sahasrara walked. It felt like hours had gone by. Virgil looked at the walls and there were images and hieroglyphics all over them. They did, however, begin to look familiar to him. As if each image was speaking to him. They continued to walk further in and finally they reached another door. This door had the seal of the crown chakra on it and an image of a cobra as well. Sahasrara walked to the door and spoke to it "Laaam, Vaaam, Raaam, Yaaam, Haaam, Auuum, AaaaH" she said. The door shook and slowly started to rise.

"Come" she said to Virgil

The two walked into what seemed to be a chamber. The chamber was filled with crystals of all sort, each representing a charka. In the center of the chamber were two seats made out of the amethyst crystal. Sahasrara led Virgil to one of the seats and they both sat down.

"Welcome to my chamber Virgil. Here is where we will have our last meeting before I let go off into the pyramid alone. You may say, this is your final stop before you enter into the real test. How are you feeling?" she asked

Virgil still in awe didn't have any words "I...I feel amazing. This place is beautiful" he said

"Why thank you" said Sahasrara "It took some time, but this chamber helps to erase all negative energy and fear that might still be clouding you before you enter into the rest of the pyramid. Tell me Virgil...have you met Kunda and Ura yet?" asked Sahasrara

Virgil looked at her and nodded "I have" he said

"Ahhh, interesting...be very careful and aware when you enter deeper into this pyramid Virgil...This is their sanctum. Even though those two energies live within every human, they are indeed very different for everyone. They know your weaknesses, your fears and will tempt you in every way. If they overcome you, they can and will snatch your spirit and see you as unworthy to be in your vessel. They can even gain control of you and you can slip into a darkness you cannot escape…but…if you find that flame inside of you, they will kneel before you and help you rise to become something your world sees as fiction…Become a King Virgil" said Sahasrara

"Woah…" said Virgil

Sahasrara reached her hand out to Virgil and Virgil grabbed her hand.

"I Sahasrara of the crown chakra, grant this young master the power of the crown and give him all access to my energy" said Sahasrara

A warm and powerful sensation moved from Virgils hand to each part of his body. Never had he felt such a power in his body before.

"You are protected" said Sahasrara

"Thank you" said Virgil

"Don't thank me…you earned this. Use it

wisely" said Sahasrara

She stood up and walked to door behind her.

"This is where we part ways young master Virgil. May the spirits and the source of all be with you" said Sahasrara

Virgil stood up and walked over to Sahasrara and hugged her

"I don't know why...but I'm being told to do this" said Virgil

Sahasrara smiled and hugged him back.

Virgil looked at the door and walked towards it. The door opened and nothing but darkness awaited him. He walked through the door and without a second thought the door closed behind him. Virgil closed his eyes and sighed "Back in darkness... again" he said

"Dark Virgil...are you with me" asked Virgil

"Always..." said Dark Virgil

"Little me...are you with me?" asked Virgil

"Always..." said little Virgil

Virgil nodded and walked in the darkness. The

path seemed to go on for a long time just as the one before. Deep from within the tunnel a low hiss came from the tunnel.

Virgil continued to walk and did not allow anything to stop him. It seemed the deeper he went into the pyramid the louder the hiss got. After walking for several minutes he finally came across a torch that sat outside of another chamber. He walked into the chamber and in the center were nine torches surrounding a small area for him to sit in.

He walked into the center and sat down on the ground. The effects of the mothers nectar drink had slowly began to take effect as he sat there.

"One last time...take me deep within" whispered Virgil

Virgil closed his eyes, took in a deep breath and held it. The hissing sound got louder and louder, until it disappeared. Virgil opened his eyes and he was sitting in front of his tree but his tree did not look the same. It had bloomed into what seemed to be a cherry blossom tree. Circulating within the tree was a strand of bright and gold DNA swirling throughout the entire tree. There waiting for him were his past child version and his inner dark version. Virgil stood up and walked towards both of them.

"Well…we meet again for the final test. Are you ready?" asked shadow Virgil

"I'm not! I dislike snakes! All of them! Why snakes?! Please explain this to me?!" shouted little Virgil

Virgil smiled and placed a hand on his little self

"We've got this…I'm ready" said Virgil

Shadow Virgil nodded and stood aside "I'll let you do the honor this time" he said

Virgil walked towards the tree and placed his hand on it "Kun, Ura, Da, Eus, Lini" said Virgil

The cheery blossom tree began to shake and vibrate the entire area

"Hehehehe! Let the real fun begin!!!" shouted Shadow Virgil

The tree began to calm itself and the small pathway ,from before, opened up.

"Come sssssss" said the serpents

"I'm gonna pass out" said little Virgil

Without a second thought, Virgil walked into the pathway.

"Can we, you know, just talk about this first?" asked little Virgil

"Ugh, stop being such a scaredy cat!" said Shadow Virgil as he picked up little Virgil and carried him on his shoulders

"Noooo! Just leave me here! Leave me here!!" shouted little Virgil.

The pathway closed and the three Virgils walked towards the serpent's room.

The doors to the chamber were still open from before and Virgil walked right through them. He walked to the center of the chamber, along with his other versions and stood in the center. Shadow Virgil dropped little Virgil who was still frightened. Virgil looked up at the throne chair and unlike last time, there was someone, cloaked of course, sitting in the chair holding the staff that was next to it.

"Who…who are you?" asked Virgil

The strange person remained silent.

"Well well well, what do we have here sssssss" said one of the serpents.

Virgil looked up and saw both of the giant cobra's slithering down from the ceiling of the chamber to the ground.

"He returned sssissster" said Kunda

"He indeed did brother" said Ura

"I wasss beginning to get bored of ssstaying inssside of thisss prissson" said Kunda

"I asss well brother...have you returned to give usss your body boy?" asked Ura

"No" said Virgil

"Mmmmm, confident isss he" said Kunda

Virgil turned to his other version "Get back inside of me" he said

"But" said Shadow Virgil

"Say less" said little Virgil

"Trust me" said Virgil

His other versions returned inside of Virgil body and he stood facing both of the serpents.

"Foolisssh move boy…they were your only help" said Ura

Ura slithered close to Virgil and looked deep within his eyes

"Mmmmmm, yesss, I know everything about you Virgil" she said

"You are weak…you lack the power to become a true man. You are nothing!" said Ura

"But…allow usss to ussse your body and we can give you everything. All of your deepessst desssiresss" said Kunda

"Richesss…Wealth…Love…Confidence…Truth…Power…You will be the most powerful being among the other humansss" said Ura

"The woman who broke your heart will come back to you…you will get that job you've alwaysss wanted…you will never have to sssuffer ever again" said Kunda

"The power of the serpents will be yours!" said both serpents

The visuals of all the serpents spoke of began to travel through Virgils mind. He felt the feeling of being that man they spoke of. He saw himself on top of the world, being wealthy, rich, free from everything and he saw his ex that he loved returning back to him. Starting a family and growing, finally being happy. Everything was perfect in that world.

"Ssssss ssso, what do you sssay Virgil? Do we have a deal?" asked Ura and Kunda

Virgil looked up at them as the serpents smiled at him.

"No" said Virgil

"Sssss you foolisssh boy! How dare you sssay no to the cosssmic ssserpentsssss!" shouted the serpents

The serpents opened their mouths and dived for Virgil prepared to eat him.

Virgil closed his eyes and held both of his hands up towards them. The serpents stopped right at the palm of his hands. Virgil placed a hand on each of the serpents.

"I say no...because none of those things really matter anymore" said Virgil

"I agree...it felt amazing. It really did...but I'm still going to be a great man without those things.

They don't define me" said Virgil

He looked up at the serpents "But with your help...I can achieve something greater than all of those things...I can achieve true peace...happiness ...and love....I believe those things are more important. Wouldn't you agree?" asked Virgil

The serpents backed away and looked at one another.

"Hmmmm, what do you sssay sssissster?" asked Kunda

Ura looked down at Virgil "I like thisss boy" she said

The serpents let out a loud hisss and let out a bright light from within them. The light was too bright for Virgil to look at so he covered his eyes. When they light began to fade, he uncovered his eyes and in front of him was another serpent. This one was a larger cobra. Its skin was bright green and its eyes were golden. It lowered itself and slowly curved around Virgil.

"Well done Virgil" said the Cobra

"I am Naga...your guardian, your protector and the true source of Kundalini and Uraeus energy" said Naga

The cobra leaned in and Virgil placed a hand on the top of its head.

"The abilites, gifts and talents promised to you before will be given to you in due time. However, there is someone else who has been dying to meet you" said Naga and turned and looked at the thrown chair.

Virgil turned and look at the person sitting in the chair. The person signaled Virgil to come towards them. Virgil nodded and began to walk to them. As Virgil approached them, he couldn't help but to feel a strange happiness come over him. As if he knew who the person was. He stopped a few feet in front of the person and waited for further instructions.

"Hmmm, if you were anyone else, I would have had you kneel before me" said the strange person who happened to be an older man.

"Have...have we met?" asked Virgil

The man chuckled "You can say that" he said

The man looked at Naga and was pleased.

"So, your Naga is green....Hmmm much love flows through your body Virgil. Just the way I intended it to be" said the man

Virgil looked at the Naga and back at the man "What?" he asked

The man stood up and he was giant. From afar he looked small but he was almost at least seven to eight feet tall.

"Uhhhh, woah...wasn't expecting that" said Virgil

The man put a hand out "Come Naga" he said

The snake slithered over to the man and he placed his palm on it.

"Naga the cobra takes the color of the chakra you most resonate with, that has impacted you the most on your journey. Yours is green which symbolizes the heart chakra. Which also means much love flows through you my boy" said the man

"Ahhh, I see" said Virgil as he also placed a hand on Naga as well.

"Naga, return back to the staff until the boy calls upon you" said the man

Naga nodded it's head "Yesss my king"

Naga shrunk it's size and split back into Kunda and Ura. The two serpents slithered to the golden staff and coiled all the up to the top of it, facing each other at the end. Their skin then changed into silver and copper. The man grabbed the staff and handed it to Virgil.

"This is now yours. You will be needing it in the future. It's very powerful so use it wisely" said the man

Virgil grabbed the staff from the man and nodded "Thank you and I will" he said

The man chuckled "Well, this is now your chamber Virgil. Anytime you need answers, come to the tree within you and into this chamber. All will be revealed to you" said the man.

Virgil nodded and looked around "I mean, that's nice and all...but you have yet to tell me who you are and why you're here" said Virgil

"Ha" laughed the man "Meet me on the outside, in the pyramid and I'll show you" he said.

He removed a hand from his cloak and Virgil realized the man's skin was...green. The man placed a finger on Virgil's forehead "Awaken" he said

Virgil blinked and he was back in the pyramid. He was holding the golden staff in his hand when he woke up and also saw that the room was no longer dark but lit with torches all around. There were giant symbols everywhere and all through the pyramid ceiling. Finally sitting in front of him was a man in ancient Egyptian clothing. He was giant, wore a large crown, with a serpent in the middle of it and the strangest thing was that his skin was green.

"Uhhhh....Ummm...Who are you?" asked Virgil

The man smiled "I've been waiting to answer that question for you since the day I chose you and you were born in that body Virgil" said the man

"I am an old ancient spirit of the ancient world …I've been called many things over the years… Many know me as Osiris…but you…you may call me Asar."

PT. 3

THE NEW BEGINNING

"Asar?" asked Virgil

Asar nodded his head "Indeed, and actually that is your name as well" he said

"I'm confused" said Virgil

Asar laughed "You will come to understand in due time... Mmmm and excuse me to by the way. The language you new humans speak is so... primitive compared to my time that is. Very... difficult" said Asar

Asar stood to his feet and it was like looking at an actual giant in the flesh.

"Come, let us talk while we walk to the final chamber" said Asar

Virgil, still in awe, nodded his head and stood to his feet.

The two began to walk together throughout the pyramid.

"You have many questions Virgil, now is the time to ask" said Asar

"I...I don't really know where to start" said Virgil

"Hahaha" laughed Asar "That's perfectly fine...we are now connected. For if you ever want to talk to me, we always can" said Asar

"Well...can you tell me something? Like anything at all?" asked Virgil

"Hmmm" thought Asar "Well...you are one of many of the chosen Kings and Queens, of the past, to rise up, heal your earth and usher in a new era of peace in the coming future" said Asar "There's so much to discuss, so much coming that I must tell you. In due time" he said

Virgil and Asar walked the pyramid halls talking

for hours. Asar told him of the past, the ancient days, the golden ages, the peace, the wars, the rise and fall of different civilizations.

"Woah…This is…a lot" said Virgil

"It is…but you asked" said Asar as he chuckled.

"I'm a King" said Virgil

"Not just any king…You are a mighty King" said Asar

"Many will try to bring you down in the future. Even those who look like you can be your worse enemy… but you must remain strong and wise. The mistakes from the past, learn from them. Be greater than all the past kings. You are love Virgil… remember that"

The two walked up to a giant door and stopped. Asar looked at Virgil and placed a hand on his shoulder.

"This is where I must leave you Virgil. You must go into this final chamber alone" said Asar

"I should have known" said Virgil

Asar placed a hand on the golden staff "if you ever need Naga or I, just look within. You know this already" said Asar

Virgil nodded as Asar vanished into the staff.

The door to the final chamber opened and Virgil walked inside. In the chamber, waiting for him, Virgil was surprised to see none other than Master Net standing in the center of the chamber.

"Master Net!" shouted Virgil as he ran over.

"Ahhh, you've made it Virgil! I've been waiting for hours!" said Master Net

"Master Net, you…you would not believe what I found out!...Did you know that I was Asar! I'm…I'm a king! A real king! And Asar, he's amazing! Tall and green, kind of weird at first, but still very…." Virgil paused his sentence and looked at Master Net

"Wait…why…why are you in here?" asked Virgil

"He's here with me" said a womans voice

A woman appeared from behind Master Net dressed in the same clothing as Asar.

"Greetings young king…I've also have waited a long time to meet you. My name is Queen Ma'at. One of the ancestors from the ancient times"

Virgil looked Ma'at up and down "Wow you're beautiful...I said that with confidence this time Master Net" he said

Ma'at smiled "Thank you young king"

Master Net walked up next to Ma'at

"Ma'at...may you give us a minute" asked Master Net

"Indeed, but we don't have much time. He'll be here soon" said Ma'at

"I know...I know" said Master Net

Ma'at walked off to the side leaving Virgil and Master Net in the center.

"What's going on Master Net?" asked Virgil

Master Net sighed "Something I now feel I should have told you months ago"

"You're leaving...aren't you?" asked Virgil

Master Net looked at Virgil "How?"

"Come on Master Net, I've seen enough movies and read enough manga's to know when the Master is about to leave the apprentice behind. I've known since earlier when we had our talk in the desert...

and still…I'm not ready" said Virgil

Master Net walked up to Virgil "No one is ever truly ready to say goodbye. We think we are, until it happens. Unlike me…you are very ready Virgil" said Master Net

Virgil looked up at Master Net

"Death…is never the end" said Virgil

"It's only just the beginning" said Master Net

The two hugged each other as if a father was saying goodbye to his son.

"Thank you…thank you for everything. You didn't have to…but I'm happy you did" said Virgil

Ma'at walked over to the two and placed her hand on Master Net

"It's time" she said

Master Net nodded "Virgil, you have to step outside of the center. It's time"

Virgil backed out of the center of the chamber and in an instant the entire room began to shake. Virgil looked up and the pyramid ceiling began to slowly open up.

"Wha...what is going on?" asked Virgil

From the ceiling, the light from the moon shined down into the center chamber.

"Ascension" whispered Master Net

Ma'at walked into the center of the chamber next to Master Net. She grabbed Master Net's hand and smiled.

"Time for you to finally go home" said Ma'at

Master Net smiled as the energy from the moon touched his skin. He then looked at Virgil grinned.

"When you begin to look inside, all the answers to the universe will no longer hide" said Master Net

"Naqi...you are finally ready" said a mans voice.

From the top of the pyramid, a giant melanated man floated down to the center of the chamber. He wasn't just in ordinary man. His presence could be felt throughout the entire chamber. He stood tall, strong and mighty. He was covered in all white garments and wore a golden cobra crown on his head.

"It's been a long time...my old friend" said the man

Master Net looked up at the tall man but could not recognize who he was.

"Apologies...but, how do I know you?" asked Master Net

Ma'at bowed before the man "He is ready my king" she said

The man smiled "Hahaha, I know he is" said the man "He is one of my students after all"

"Students?" said Master Net

Virgil slowly began to walk towards the center

"Ahhh, the young neteru, Master Virgil. I've been waiting to meet you as well. I'm expecting a lot of great things from you" said the man

"Are...are you who I think you are?" asked Virgil

The giant man turned and looked at Virgil

"I am" said the man "I am King Anu...King of Nibiru and King of the Nubian people known as the Annunaqi...nice to meet you young king. Our time here is short, we have much work that need to be done in the cosmos. It's time I bring my young apprentice with me this time" said King Anu

He turned and looked at Master Net "Let us go, my friend"

Waves of energy slowly came down from the heavens and hit Master Net. The energy felt warm, calm and peaceful. Master Net closed his eyes, smiled and took in one final breath "Farewell" he whispered

His body slowly began to turn into ash and dust until there was nothing left but his garments. Standing there, where Master Net was, was a bright green spirit. It looked at Virgil, then at King Anu and finally at Ma'at.

"Ma'at?" said the spirit

"Yes...it's good to see you again Thoth...my King"

Ma'at walked over and wrapped her arms around the spirit. The two slowly began to lift up into the sky along with King Anu.

"We will be meeting again very soon Master Virgil...and tell Asar I said hello" said King Anu

The spirit of Thoth looked down at Virgil "We shall meet again young master" said Thoth.

Virgil watched as all three lifted up into the heavens and the pyramid ceiling began to close, until he was all that was left. The final door opened from the pyramid that led to the outside. Virgil walked to the door and outside where the others were waiting.

As Virgil walked out, he felt tears falling from his eyes. Virgil saw Master Aynu and walked up towards him and hugged him.

"I know...I know" said Master Aynu

Sahasrara walked up to Virgil and placed a hand on his shoulder.

"Master Virgil...this...is the way. You are now ready to follow this path. It's your turn now" said Sahasrara

The chakra sisters walked up to Virgil and said their farewells. Muladhara ran up and hugged him "I'm always with you Virgil" she whispered.

As she began to walk towards her sisters Sahasrara stopped Muladhara.

"Actually sister...I have a request for you" she said

"Request?" asked Muladhara

"Indeed…I am sending Anahata on a mission elsewhere to help another on their journey…do you mind staying behind with Virgil?" asked Sahasrara

"YES!" shouted Muladhara

"Good…but you cannot be in human form" said Sahasrara

"…what?" asked Muladhara

Her other sisters laughed. Kema walked up to Muladhara.

"You already know what to do sister" said Kema

Muladhara rolled her eyes "Fine" she said

She used her energy and shifted her body into the form of a black cat

"I don't understand how you've gone thousands of years like this Anahata" said Muladhara

"That suits you well sister. Just as Anahata stood beside Master Net, you will do the same with Master Virgil now" said Sahasrara

Muladhara walked over and climbed onto Virgils shoulder.

"I am still Brya to you" said Muladhara

Virgil rubbed her on her head and looked up into the stary sky.

"So…what's next?" asked Virgil

"You tell us Master Virgil" said Master Aynu

As Virgil gazed into the starry sky, six shooting stars flew through the sky. Virgil chuckled and put a hand on his forehead.

"Honestly…I'm ready to go back and make some changes on my home. Too many people are suffering on my earth. Too much pain, too much sadness, too much hurt, too much corruption…too much chaos. There isn't a balance anymore…and it's time I be the change…How will I do it? I don't have those answers…but I'm going to make it happen…one way or another…I have a voice now…I have spirit that wants to speak to the people that have been suffering…and I'm going to be one of many to help those people rise. Rise from the ashes…and back into the kingdom of sun…This, is the new Beginning" said Virgil

End…

Epilogue

The rays from the sun shined down onto the scared forest. Master Aynu and Virgil were inside of Master Nets hut going through his old journals, while drinking some tea.

"Boy...Master Net really record everything he's been through over the years" said Virgil

"Indeed he has...ahhh look at this!" said Master Aynu

He was holding up an old picture of Master Net and someone else standing to next him, in front of the Great Pyramid of Giza.

"Hmmm, who is that with Master Net?" asked Virgil

Aynu looked at the picture again "ohh...that is...one of Master Nets old students" he said.

Virgil grabbed the picture and saw that the person was a man that looked no older than he did, but the picture was really old, so the man had to be of some age by now.

"Did you know him?" asked Virgil

"I did...unfortunately" said Aynu

"Why do you say that?" asked Virgil

Aynu grabbed the photo from Virgil and placed it back into the journal where he found it.

"Some things are better off left in the past Virgil... this is one of them" said Aynu

Brya, while in her cat form, was walking around the hut looking nosily at all the crystals Master Net had collected over the years. Since she was the guardian of the root chakra she took a special interest in all of the different red crystals he had. There was one crystal, however, that was very peculiar. It was emerald and had nine different carvings all over it. Brya had knowledge of almost every crystal that could be found on the earth, but she had no knowledge of this one. As she approached it, the crystal let off a loud screeching noise. Brya jumped back and ran over towards Virgil and Aynu.

"What did you get into Brya?" asked Virgil

"Don't blame me, I'm sorry I like shiny things" said Brya

Virgil walked over to where the loud screech had come from and saw the crystal. As he reached for it, the crystal reacted differently this time. It let out a calming and soothing aura that filled the entire hut.

"Master Aynu, what is this?" asked Virgil

Aynu walked over to observe the crystal

"I've…never seen this before. It's very odd but it seems to respond well to you" said Aynu

As Virgil continued to observe the crystal he noticed that there was something else in the area where the crystal was. He reached down and grabbed what happened to be a small black book. He opened the book to the first page and saw that there was a message from Master Net left there. The message read "To my apprentice…if you have discovered this book, then you have also discovered the crystal I left behind as well. Both items are about to help serve you and the next phase on your journey. The crystal is an ancient artifact known as the Emerald Seeker. Its purpose is to help locate the nine rulers of ancient earth and bring them together in a time of need. I was given this crystal by Queen Ma'at, months after you had started your training with me. She knew only you would be able to use it when the time was right. Now, in your hands you are holding a black book with very secretive information that I have obtained from over the years. In this book, you will find four other individuals who are just like you, and who are either about to begin or have started their journey into this life. To my apprentice, who now will be known as Master and King. Find your Neteru family, and finally bring everyone together" signed Neteru Master Naqi

Virgil looked up at Master Aynu

"Don't look at me, go through the book!" he said

Virgil began flipping through the book and saw that there were indeed pictures of eight people throughout the book. Four melanated women and five melanated men. The crystal began to pulse through each picture that he saw.

"Well...it seems like your journey is about to become much bigger" said Brya

Virgil opened the last page of the book and saw a picture of a woman with a map next to her, along with the caption "Every King needs a Queen, Find Her"

Virgil looked at Master Aynu and he shook his head

"Don't look at me...this is your book, your journey...I am to protect the forest. You must go alone" he said

"But.." said Virgil

"But nothing! You are a young master and a young king...you will figure it out...now go Virgil" said Aynu

Virgil sighed and walked outside of the hut along with Brya. He looked in the back of the book again to see the picture of the woman.

"No name, no location, no direction...this shall be fun, don't you think Brya?" asked Virgil

"Come...let's go find her" said Brya

The sun shined down upon them, and as the rays came down the emerald crystal began to shine. It gravitated from Virgil's hand into the air and shot a light that pointed North. The next chapter had finally begun.

About the Author

Michael F. Lawrence Jr. was born in Warner Robins, Georgia and raised in LaGrange, Georgia. He is the son to Sharee and Michael Lawrence Sr. and the big brother to Sydney Lawrence. He is a Fort Valley State University graduate with a bachelor's in health and Physical Education and a Masters in School Counseling Education. Michael's inspiration for writing comes from his love for anime, spirituality, ancient history and Studio Ghibli films. What inspired him to pursue the art of writing his own book was reading Paulo Coelho's book The Alchemist. The idea of following life's path and journey left a mark on him. Now he seeks to share his own creative talents with the world and assist people of all ages to discover their true potential.

Finding Me
By: LaKeisha Coleman

I once traveled to the bottom of a wishing well

wondering what I'd see

I was wishing I would find more

Never thought I'd find just me

I wanted to be like everyone else

And possibly find happiness too

Instead, I realized that all I need

Was hidden inside of me

Not you

I realized I had strengths that would
carry me along the way

I realized that even my weaknesses would be
appreciated someday

I realized that all of my failures were in
place to help me grow

I realized that fears were simply misconceptions
of things I didn't know

As I came to the surface of the well, I was not
disappointed by what I did not see

Because instead of finding everyone else

I found love for me

Discussion Question

What can you do right now to change your reality and make your life more meaningful?

_____

_____

_____

_____

_____

_____

_____

_____

_____

_____

_____

_____

_____

_____

_____

Asé
Peace, Power, Love and Light Family.

Made in the USA
Columbia, SC
20 April 2021